LOST BOY

LOST BOY

Shelley Hrdlitschka

ORCA BOOK PUBLISHERS

Library and Archives Canada Cataloguing in Publication

Hrdlitschka, Shelley, 1956–, author
Lost boy / Shelley Hrdlitschka.

Issued in print and electronic formats.
ISBN 978-1-4598-1637-4 (softcover).—ISBN 978-1-4598-1638-1 (pdf).—
ISBN 978-1-4598-1639-8 (epub)

I. Title.

PS8565.R44L67 2018   JC813'.54   C2017-907676-0
C2017-907677-9

First published in the United States, 2018
Library of Congress Control Number: 2018933726

Summary: In this work of fiction for young adults, a teenage boy is banished from
his polygamous community after he is caught kissing a girl.

MIX
Paper from
responsible sources
FSC® C016245

*Orca Book Publishers is dedicated to preserving the environment and has
printed this book on Forest Stewardship Council® certified paper.*

Orca Book Publishers gratefully acknowledges the support for its publishing
programs provided by the following agencies: the Government of Canada through
the Canada Book Fund and the Canada Council for the Arts, and the Province of British
Columbia through the BC Arts Council and the Book Publishing Tax Credit.

Edited by Sara Cassidy
Cover illustration by Marie Bergeron
Author photo by Leslie Thomas

ORCA BOOK PUBLISHERS
orcabook.com

Printed and bound in Canada.

21   20   19   18   •   4   3   2   1

For my Maui Sistas—
for nourishing me in so many ways.

Part One

One

"Jon! Noooo! Please don't go."

Celeste's cries follow me as I pick my way across the rocky beach along the river. Her desperation messes with my heart. I brush away tears, but I won't look back. I cram my fists into my pockets and will myself to keep walking— away from her, away from my family, away from everything I've ever known.

"Joonnnn!"

I begged her to come with me, argued that we could escape together, but she just couldn't do it.

A river rock rolls under my foot, and my hands spring free from my pockets. I catch myself, but it's too late—pain shoots up my leg. I've twisted my ankle. I can't stop to tend it. The hesitation could be my undoing. I straighten my shoulders, clench my jaw and keep walking.

The sound of the rushing river drowns out Celeste's voice, but the taste of her lips on mine is still fresh, as is the full-body rush brought on by those kisses.

The Prophet always told us boys to stay away from girls, to treat them as though they were poisonous snakes. If we're ever worthy of being assigned a first wife, well then, those snakes miraculously turn into girls. But now that I know what a girl's kisses taste like, what she feels like in my arms, there's no going back. It's no wonder he worked so hard to keep boys and girls apart. I'd gladly have taken Celeste to be my wife for "time and all eternity," but that is not how the Prophet does things. He's the one to choose.

The stones have graduated to boulders. It's becoming more difficult to trek downstream, but there's only one unpaved road out of Unity, and it would create suspicion if anyone saw me walking there. I'll stick to the river until it winds under the main road to Springdale.

I've known for months that I'd eventually leave Unity. My struggles with the rules of our faith have made it impossible to stay. I just didn't know that today would be the day.

I finally reach the bridge that spans the river. Over my head, traffic whooshes past. I scramble up the bank, ignoring the stabs of pain in my ankle, and step onto the paved road that leads to Springdale.

I could still be spotted by someone from Unity, but it's unlikely. While Celeste and I met at the beach this morning, the rest of the community was at a memorial service. Everyone should still be at the church.

I walk along the shoulder of the road. Cars and trucks rumble past, and the sun beats down on me. Will I really burn in hell for leaving the faith? I swallow hard. There's no turning back now.

The heat is becoming unbearable, and my ankle is throbbing hard. A truck roars up behind me. I turn and stick out my thumb. The truck driver flicks on his blinkers and pulls his rig over to the shoulder of the road. I limp up to the cab, haul myself onto the running board and open the door. A blast of cool, air-conditioned air hits my face.

The driver checks me over. "Where are you headed, son?"

The Prophet says that all outsiders—or gentiles, as we call them—are evil, but this guy doesn't seem scary. He's about my dad's age and looks like he has spent a lot of time in the sun.

"Springdale."

"Hop in."

He pulls the rig back onto the road and looks me over again. "Are you a polyg?" he asks, not unkindly.

Polyg is a shortened version of *polygamist*. Only gentiles use it. On my rare trips into Springdale, teenagers have said it under their breath as they pass me on the sidewalk. My father told me to pay no attention. After all, we were the chosen ones, the only people who would go to heaven. At one time I'd felt smug, knowing that my family was special, even if we stood out because of our clothing and our large families. Dad has five wives and a large mob of children.

"I was," I tell the driver.

His brow springs up. "Well now."

"Uh-huh." I'm trying to get my head around what I've said. *Was.* If I'm leaving a faith community that practices polygamy, then I'm an apostate. Apostates are no better than filthy animals.

"Then I guess you can lose some of the layers," the driver says, glancing at my best go-to-church clothing.

"I'm okay."

His face softens. He fiddles with a dial on the dashboard and turns up the air-conditioning. I undo the top button of my long-sleeved shirt and lean my head back on the seat.

The driver turns up the volume on the radio. The music is unfamiliar. I listen closely, both appalled and intrigued by the lyrics:

Don't stop now
Oh baby, oh baby
Feel it
Move it
Rock it
Oh, oh baby
Don't stop now

We were only permitted to listen to spiritual music in Unity, but on those occasions when Jimmy showed up late at night for a visit, we boys would sneak off and sit in the cab of his pickup truck and listen to music he called rock or punk or pop. I liked the music, but it's all still new to me.

"Boys like you, the ones who leave places like Unity, are called Lost Boys," the driver says.

"So I've heard."

I close my eyes and try to rest, but as the distance between this truck and Unity grows wider, the reality of what I'm doing sinks in. I remember Jimmy saying that, for him, escaping was like staring Satan in the face and telling him to go fuck himself. I was impressed at the time, but am I really that brave? Do I want to be just another Lost Boy?

I think of Celeste, and a deep sorrow washes over me. I can still hear her pleading for me to stay, even though she knew it was impossible after we'd been found out.

"You know anyone in Springdale?" the driver asks.

I blink my eyes open. We're passing warehouses and industrial parks, which means we're getting close to town. I reach into my pocket for the slip of paper with Jimmy's phone number on it. It's there, as always, just in case. I used the number yesterday to call him for help with someone else. Taviana. I flatten the scrap on my knee.

"Need a phone?" the driver asks, glancing at the number. He reaches for his mobile on the truck console.

"Thanks," I say.

While I enter the number, the driver pulls the rig into an empty parking lot. The phone rings four times, then goes to messages. I hand the phone back. "My friend must be at work," I say.

"Well, the park is just down that street there," the driver says, pointing. "Beside the river. It's where all the young people hang out after school. Maybe you could meet some of them, figure out where you might find a place to stay."

"Thanks, sir. I'll go straight there."

He smiles at that. "You seem like a nice kid. I wish you well."

I'm astonished at the kindness in the man's eyes. So much for the Prophet's lessons about gentiles. Jimmy always says the Prophet was lying, and now I'm seeing it for myself.

I shoulder open the cab door and step to the ground, being careful not to land on my sore ankle. When I look back to say goodbye, the driver is taking his wallet from his pocket. He pulls out a bill. "Buy yourself a T-shirt and some shorts," he says, handing it to me. "If there's anything left over, you can get a burger."

I take the bill reluctantly and then look at the number in the corner. One hundred dollars! "Are you sure?"

He nods. "I am. Just be sure to pay it forward when you're back on your feet. Best of luck to you. It's not going to be easy."

I wave as the man maneuvers his eighteen-wheeler back onto the road. He blows the horn twice.

I study the crisp bill in my hand. I've never seen so much money, even though I've worked in construction for three years. Almost all the money I made was paid directly to the church or to my father.

It's a short walk to the park. Mothers minding their small children on the playground equipment eye me suspiciously. I decide to head to the river. There I sprawl under a massive weeping willow tree and listen to the rushing water and think about what I've done.

Only two hours ago, I lay by this same river with Celeste in my arms. Now it's possible that I'll never see her again.

It's midafternoon, according to where the sun is. The truck driver thought I should talk to kids my age and figure out where to stay, but I know there's not a chance they'll talk to me. Surely he knew that. I'm a polyg, and gentiles are not known for being nice to polygs. My only hope is to contact Jimmy.

I reach into my pocket to feel that the money is still there. My throat is parched, and I'm hungry. Food and water would be so good right now. They wouldn't cost much either. But if I can't get in touch with Jimmy, I may really need the money later.

Jimmy is my only connection outside of Unity. He was the one who talked me into leaving. He convinced me that I had a choice, that I didn't need to live the way my family does. For a long time I resisted, but more and more I've also begun to question the Prophet. Some of his teachings just don't make sense.

The sun's glare is intense. I close my eyes. When I open them again, the sun has moved much farther to the west. I must have fallen asleep. Nearby, a guy is squatting beside the river. He's wearing shorts. His torso is bare, and his shirt hangs from his back pocket. His skin is light brown. He stays crouched for five, ten minutes, hardly moving, creating something with the river rocks. Finally he stands and stretches.

He has balanced a tower of stones in a way that looks impossible. They should just topple over.

He starts working on something I recognize—an inuksuk, a figure of a human made from stones. That's when I make the connection. He must be the same guy who has been building inuksuit near Unity. Celeste and I discovered the rock men—as we called them—on the beach and liked them so much that we began building our own. Soon there was a whole community of them.

I stand and walk toward him. He turns when he hears the stones crunch under my feet.

A friendly smile lights up his face. "You must be from Unity," he says, taking in my long-sleeved shirt, pants and lace-up shoes. His comment isn't derogatory, just curious.

"Was," I say for the second time that afternoon. "Not anymore."

He tips his head but doesn't say anything else, just returns to building his inuksuk.

"Are you from Springdale?" I ask.

"My parents live here now, but I didn't grow up here. I'm just staying with them until I figure out what to do next with my life." He reaches for a rock. "What about you? Are you still in school?"

"No. Construction. I don't know what I'm going to do next either."

"There are so many options, aren't there?"

I can only shrug.

"What do you like doing?" he asks.

"I don't know. Never given it much thought."

He adds a head to his inuksuk and stands back to admire his work. Just then a cell phone in his pocket pings. He pulls it out and looks at the screen. "Gotta go," he says. He sticks out his hand. "I'm Craig, by the way. Maybe I'll see you around."

"Jon," I say, shaking his hand. "Yeah, maybe."

Craig begins to jog across the beach.

"Craig!" I call to his back.

"Yeah?" He swings around to look at me, still trotting backward.

"May I make a quick call on your phone?"

"Oh, sure." He jogs back and hands it to me.

I pull the slip of paper out of my pocket and press the numbers.

Two

"Oh. My. God. Jon!"

The shock on her face makes me smile. "Hi, Taviana."

Taviana drops her book, jumps out of her chair, flies across the small room and nearly knocks me over as she throws her arms around me.

I'm pleased with this warm welcome, but I don't hug her back. Aside from my mom and my littlest sisters, Celeste is the only girl I've ever hugged, and hugging her was breaking all the rules.

When Taviana finally lets me go, I notice a couple of guys standing behind her in the kitchen doorway. Matthew and Selig. I don't know them well. We aren't related, which is unusual when you come from Unity, but I know that Jimmy used to meet them late at night too. The way I heard it, Matthew was dropped off on the side of the highway by his mother and told never to return. Apparently he was caught wearing a short-sleeved shirt while doing construction work in the summer. It was the final transgression of many.

Like me, Selig left voluntarily, and not long ago. Jimmy must have convinced him, too, that with his history of questioning the Prophet, it wasn't likely he'd get assigned one wife, let alone three, which is how many you need to get into heaven. And if we weren't going to heaven with the rest of them, what was the point in staying?

"Hi," I say to Matthew and Selig, giving a little wave.

They both smile shyly.

"Hello, Jon." A woman squeezes past Matthew and Selig and shakes my hand. "I'm Abigail. This is my home."

I nod, feeling incredibly awkward.

"Jimmy's told me about you."

Abigail looks exactly as I'd pictured her: stout, with a no-nonsense expression on a bulldog face. Her dark hair, streaked with gray, is pulled back into a thick braid that hangs to her waist. She once lived in Unity too, and she still hasn't cut her hair, which is the custom of the women. But her knee-length pants and short-sleeved blouse definitely wouldn't be worn in Unity.

Jimmy answered my call from the river and immediately drove over to pick me up. He told me that Abigail was expecting me.

"Have you had any dinner, Jon?" she asks now.

I'm tempted to lie. It seems rude to arrive hungry, but before I can open my mouth, my stomach releases a loud rumble.

I slap a hand to my middle and feel my face burn. The boys hoot with laughter.

"Taviana, please scramble up some eggs for Jon. And boys," she says to Matthew and Selig, "you get back to your homework. Jimmy, you can give Taviana a hand in the kitchen. I think the dishwasher needs unloading."

Jimmy meets my eyes and smiles. He warned me that the boys here help with the women's chores.

"I wish I'd known you were coming today," Abigail says, settling herself into a rocking chair. "Taviana made us an amazing meal, but we ate every scrap of it. I would have saved you some. You don't have a suitcase or a bag?"

"No, I left kind of…suddenly."

"What happened?"

There's no reason to lie to this woman. She's likely heard it all before. "I was caught with a girl. Her sister saw us together, and she's the type who'd go straight to their father."

"You didn't go back to say goodbye to your mother?"

My mother. All day I've managed to block out thoughts of her. I can't imagine never seeing her again. It was because of her—and Celeste, of course—that I stayed as long as I did.

A lump swells in my throat. "Everyone was at a funeral when I left." My voice is wobbly. "I wouldn't have been able to speak to her alone."

"Who died?"

"Colleen Musser."

"Joseph's oldest girl?"

I nod. "She died giving birth."

"Oh no. How old was she?"

"Sixteen. A year younger than me." And a year older than Celeste.

Abigail slumps in her chair. "If only I could help the girls too."

I look around the small room, trying to steady myself. The walls are covered with framed photos, mostly of kids from Unity, judging by their clothes. I'd heard that when Abigail left Unity, she had to leave all her children behind. A few of the older boys eventually followed her out, but not her daughters. Not yet anyway.

"Who's your father?"

"Martin Nielsson."

"One of the decent ones." I glance at her, surprised. I assumed that she'd hate all the men in Unity after what they put her through. "Your mother won't sleep well tonight," she murmurs.

I don't trust my voice to answer.

"And I'm assuming you need a place to stay?"

I nod.

Taviana and Jimmy clatter back into the room. Taviana places a tray with a plate of eggs and toast, muffins and a bowl of fruit on the coffee table in front of me. Jimmy follows with a large glass of milk. He and Taviana then settle down on either side of me on the creaky couch.

"While you eat, I'll go over the house rules," Abigail says. "They're fresh in my mind—I went over them with Taviana just last night."

I force myself to eat slowly, politely, and not gobble the food down, but it's hard. I'm so hungry.

"As Jimmy probably told you, I take in kids who have left Unity and need a place to live. The authorities recognize the service I provide for you guys, so they turn a blind eye when it comes to laws about legal guardianship and all that."

The muffins are warm. Slabs of golden margarine melt into them. I'm having trouble focusing on Abigail's words.

"Rule number one. You must attend high school until you graduate."

I swallow another mouthful of food. "I haven't been to school since I was fourteen."

"We'll help you get caught up. It was the same for the other two." She glances toward the kitchen. "And they're doing okay."

She doesn't sound completely convinced. I keep eating. I'm fine with that rule. I always wanted to finish school anyway, and maybe even go to college. That would never have been an option in Unity.

"Everyone pitches in with the cooking and cleaning," Abigail continues. "I provide a place for you to live, but it's not a hotel. The curfew is ten thirty on school nights, midnight on weekends. If you can, I encourage you to work part-time while you attend school, so you can contribute to your room and board. I expect common courtesy and good manners at all times. No drugs, alcohol or smoking. We respect each other's belongings, and we each attend a church service of our choice."

I look up from my food, surprised.

"I may have left Unity," Abigail says, looking directly at me, "but I did not lose my faith in a higher power. It is my hope that the members of this family—and that's what we are, a family—will find strength in God's love, just as I do.

"This is also not a flop house," she continues. "If you bring someone over to sleep, you check with me first, as Jimmy did tonight. And last night." She looks at Taviana. "Boys and girls will occupy separate bedrooms. Occasionally we have to double up."

"More eggs?" Taviana interrupts, glancing at my clean plate.

I take a banana and settle back. "No thanks, but that was so good. What was that stuff on top of the eggs? It was delicious."

"Salsa."

Salsa. I'll have to remember that. It sounds exotic.

"Any questions, Jon?" Abigail asks.

My belly is full, and Jimmy and Taviana are on either side of me, their shoulders pressing into mine. Maybe things really will work out. I might even be able to get word to Celeste to join us.

I shake my head. "No questions. I really appreciate you helping me out this way."

"You're welcome." Abigail's voice is soft. She rocks in her chair. "If I can't raise my children, at least I can help those of you who want to find your own way." She stares at me for another moment. I feel that she's sizing me up. "I must be honest with you, Jon. Although I have helped a few boys, the success rate hasn't been great."

The room becomes still. Abigail sighs. "If you follow these simple rules, I promise to support you while you make the transition. But it's never easy. Be aware of that. There will be challenges."

The truck driver said much the same thing.

"Okay, then." Abigail hauls herself out of her chair. "Let's get you settled in. The boys will find some clothes for you. You'll have to take a basement room, because all the others are full. Tomorrow I'll call the school and make an appointment to discuss your placement. It's hard to start school at this point in the year, but maybe they can do an assessment and give you some material to study over the summer."

As I follow her out of the room, I can't believe that last night I was in Unity, at home, saying Sunday prayers with my family and thinking that the week ahead was going to be just like the last one, and the one before that—days of nothing but work, prayer and the odd glimpse of and secretive meeting with Celeste.

The toilet flushes upstairs, and floorboards creak as everyone gets ready for bed. I hang up the clothes the boys gave me earlier. I wouldn't take their shorts and T-shirts, so they gave me the clothes they still had from Unity.

"I'll give you a week before you're wearing shorts," Jimmy had said.

"Three days," Matthew bet. "What do you say, Selig?"

Selig just shrugged. "Wear whatever makes you comfortable, Jon."

I sit on the bottom bunk and look around. Other than the bed, there's only a chest of drawers and a lone chair in the corner. As in the living room, the walls are covered in framed photos. A small, high window is shuttered. I wonder about the last Lost Boy who used this room.

I am the oldest of my siblings, so I likely had my own bedroom when I was a baby. I don't remember that though. I don't recall a time when I didn't share my room and bed with at least three brothers. I've always longed for my own space, away from the constant roughhousing and mess of my brothers, but now that I have it, I feel incredibly alone.

Jimmy appears in the doorway. "Can I come in?"

"Yeah. Of course." I try not to show how glad I am to see him.

"You okay?"

"Yep," I say, even though I feel like crap. Gone is the warm and fuzzy feeling I experienced in the living room. Now I'm really struggling to keep it together.

Jimmy sits in the chair. "So what happened today?" It was the question he didn't ask when he picked me up from the park.

"I got caught with Celeste." Was that just this morning? It feels like days ago.

When Celeste and I started meeting, we'd just talk, sharing our doubts about our faith. Sometimes we built rock men on the beach, but more recently we'd spent our time in each other's arms. That's what we were doing when Nanette found us. That's when I faced my choice—leave voluntarily or be banished in disgrace. "I begged Celeste to come too, but, well, you know."

"Yeah. It's harder for the girls."

"I know, but she could be with me here, now!"

"I had one of my sisters convinced, even had her here for a few days, but she went back."

"What do you think they'll do to Celeste?" I ask, though I don't really want to know.

"Probably marry her off as fast as they can."

I can't bear to think about that. "Why did Abigail say the success rate of those who leave is so low? What did she mean?"

Jimmy frowns. "Ask me that again in six months," he says quietly.

I shoot him a look. "You only ever told us how much better it is here. How we'd have choices. And could have girlfriends, and do whatever we want. You never mentioned there'd be *challenges*."

Jimmy doesn't say anything. The toilet upstairs flushes again. We sit, deep in our own thoughts. Finally he stands. "Abigail and I work tomorrow," he says. "The boys will be in school, but you can hang out with Taviana. She'll be here all day."

In Unity, we didn't "hang out." Idle hands are the tools of the devil, they say. It will be weird to have a day where I don't have to do anything. I nod and go back to staring at the floor.

Jimmy gives my shoulder a light punch before he turns to leave. I wish he'd stay and sleep in the top bunk. I don't want to be alone.

"Hey, Jimmy?" I say.

"Yeah?"

"Thanks for everything. You know?"

He smiles. "You're welcome. And you know what?"

"What?"

"You're going to be okay."

That lump in my throat instantly returns. "Goodnight" is all I can choke out.

I climb into bed and pull the blankets up to my neck. It's cool in the basement.

I think of Celeste and wonder if she's thinking of me. Jimmy is right—she probably will be married soon. Her father already told her that the Prophet was preparing to receive a message from God about just that.

I hope he didn't hurt her when Nanette told him what we were doing. I know about the strap he keeps in his barn.

Three

Taviana knows how to make herself useful at Abigail's. She cleans the kitchen after breakfast, puts in a load of laundry for the boys, and now she's baking something.

I have no idea how to help her. I've never worked in the kitchen—my sisters and mothers did that. I worked in the yard, and when I turned fourteen, I began work in construction full time. If Abigail needed a house framed, well, I could do that.

It's a beautiful morning. My ankle feels much better, so I step into the long and narrow backyard. A basketball hoop without a net is attached to the side of an old garage. Various balls and a Frisbee lie in the yard. Where there was once a lawn, there is now only scrubby soil with green tufts. Dead bushes line a dilapidated fence.

I find an old basketball that's inflated enough to at least make shots. I bounce it a few times and shoot for the basket.

It sails in, as does my second attempt. I glance at the kitchen window to see if Taviana is watching. Nope. Making the shots isn't as satisfying when there's no one around to see. In Unity there are always at least a dozen kids hanging around the basketball hoops on the school playground. School kids. I haven't played since I left school.

I wander around the yard, picking up the abandoned balls and Frisbees and storing them neatly under the stairs. Then I pull out the dead shrubs and make a pile in the back corner of the yard. A couple of fence boards have fallen over, so I straighten them, then find tools in the garage to make repairs. After about an hour the yard looks much better. With a coat of paint on the fence and on the garage, it might even look respectable.

"Do you think Abigail would like a vegetable garden?" I ask Taviana as she peers into the oven, checking on a pan of cookies. "I could build raised beds. The season is right."

"Cool idea, Jon. Why don't you ask her when she gets home tonight?"

I agree to do that, but it doesn't help me figure out what to do with the rest of my day. "Would she mind if I watched her TV?"

Taviana smiles. "Of course not. That's what TVs are for." She tilts her head and studies me. "Have you ever watched one?"

"My dad keeps one in his closet that he hardly ever brings out. He says it's there in case of an emergency, though I don't know how a TV would help in emergencies."

"Daytime TV isn't all that good," Taviana says, showing me how to use the remote control. "But go ahead."

Taviana explains the difference between movies, talk shows and something she calls sitcoms. I like the cartoons and the commercials best. Who knew there were so many things to buy?

When Matthew and Selig bang through the door, I glance at the clock. I can't believe it. I've been watching the TV for five hours! Taviana slid a sandwich and plate of cookies in front of me at one point, and told me she was heading into the town center to apply for a library card, but I hardly remember that.

"Anything good on?" Matthew asks, plunking himself down beside me.

"What do you consider good?"

"WWF."

"What's that?"

"Wrestling."

"It's not really wrestling," Selig says. He's standing in the kitchen doorway with a cookie in his hand. "It's all scripted."

"Whatever," Matthew says. "It's still wrestling. They're real moves, and those are real injuries."

"It's stupid. The outcomes are fixed. How's that a sport?"

"It's sport crossed with entertainment," Matthew says. "And believe me, Jon, it's entertaining. Just wait."

A women's-underwear commercial comes on.

"Now *that* would give the Prophet a heart attack," Matthew says, his eyes glued to the screen.

Like mine. Like Selig's.

Selig takes another cookie from the plate on the coffee table. "Wrong," he says. "The Prophet finished high school and went to college. I bet he watched lots of TV. That's why he forbids it." He motions to the TV, where a man and a woman are sitting on a white sand beach, drinking beer. The woman is practically naked. My eyes must be huge. "How could we keep sweet if we're exposed to that stuff?"

"Keeping sweet" is all the Prophet ever talks about.

Taviana enters the room. I didn't even know she'd come home. "You guys might want to look like you're doing homework when Abigail gets back," she says. "Or chores. Dinner's ready. Can I borrow your novel again, Selig?"

She's made dinner already? I really did zone out. I turn off the TV and watch Selig take a novel from his backpack. "You read novels in high school?" I ask. Novels, like newspapers and magazines, are banned in Unity. The Prophet told us that reading them would cause us to take on the evil spirit of the authors.

"Yeah. We're supposed to," Selig says. "In class we discuss the ideas in them. I'm not much of a reader though. You're going to tell me what this one's about, right, Tavi?"

"Maybe," Taviana says, grinning.

He snatches the novel away from her and puts it behind his back. "I won't share if you're not going to help me."

Taviana tries to reach around him, and they wrestle for a moment. Eventually she gives up. "Okay, okay," she says, laughing. She holds out her hand for the book, and Selig returns it to her.

I watch this exchange, amazed by how easily Selig can horse around with a girl who is not his sister.

★　★　★

"Could I plant a vegetable garden in the backyard?"

Abigail is eating with gusto, clearly enjoying the meal Taviana made. "That's a lovely idea, Jon," she answers. She swirls a broccoli floret in her mashed potatoes. "But I don't know that the soil out there would be any good."

"I would build some raised beds and fill them with soil from a nursery."

"You'd know how to do that?"

"Yeah. I've built them before. And if I had some paint, I could put a coat on the fence and on the garage too."

Abigail doesn't answer right away. She takes a piece of bread from the basket and cleans her plate with it. Then she leans back in her chair and sighs. "I appreciate your offer, Jon. Only I don't have the cash for those supplies right now. I'm saving to buy the boys a computer. Everything else seems to go to rent and food."

"If we grew our own food, we would save money in the long run."

"Yep. Good economics. But the harvest would be months away, and I don't have the cash for supplies right now."

No one around the table makes eye contact with me. Money must be a taboo subject.

"I have one hundred dollars," I tell her. "I was going to give it to you for my keep, but maybe it could go toward the garden."

"And I could bring home some scrap lumber from the job site I'm working at," Jimmy says. "A lot gets wasted on big projects. Paint too, I'm guessing. I'll check with my supervisor."

Abigail smiles at him. The tension in the room melts away. "You know what they say at church—God provides. That would be wonderful if you could check on those supplies, Jimmy. And Jon, save your money for the soil and seeds. This might work out."

"Where did you get the money?" Selig asks. I'm helping him load the dishwasher. I've never actually seen one before. Some of the families in Unity have them, but we never did. He takes out the plate I've just put in and repositions it. "You can load more when you stack them this way."

I tell him about the truck driver. "He told me to pay it forward. What does that mean?"

"I think it means that when someone does something nice for you, you're supposed to do something nice for someone else. Not necessarily the same thing, but you give them something they need. And then they have to pay it forward too. It's a way of making the world a nicer place."

"Are those the kind of ideas you get from novels?"

His laugh is more of a snort. "I guess. But I like that one."

I take the tea towel off the handle on the oven door and dry the pots. Selig shows me where they're stored. This kitchen work's not so complicated after all.

★　★　★

The boys return to their homework after dinner. Taviana is reading her novel. Abigail has set up a sewing machine in the living room and is working her way through a basket of mending.

"Want to go for a ride around town?" Jimmy asks me, shaking a set of car keys in my face.

We climb into his pickup truck and pull out of Abigail's driveway. The evening is warm, and Jimmy waves at some little kids playing Kick the Can on the quiet street. They chase the pickup, yelling, "Jimmy! Jimmy!"

Older people sit on the front steps of their small but well-cared-for homes. They also wave as we drive by.

"Where do you want to go?" Jimmy asks.

"Where *is* there to go?"

"Depends what you want to do. We could see a movie, check out the park…"

Those sound like good choices. But just driving around with no destination in mind feels good too. I've never experienced such freedom. I roll down the window and stick out my elbow.

"Or I could take you to meet some of my friends." Jimmy glances over at me. "But they're mostly older than you."

"How old are *you*, anyway?" I've never thought to ask. All I know is he's older than me.

"Twenty-one."

"Really?"

"Uh-huh. Does that seem ancient to you?"

"Not really."

"You figure I should be married with a couple of rug rats, right?" He grins and punches me in the arm.

"No. But, well, why are you still living with Abigail? You've got a job and everything."

"True. But the rent's cheap at Abigail's, and I'm saving up for college. Construction work's okay, but I can't see myself doing it when I'm forty."

I know what he means. I've had quite a few work-related injuries already. It probably gets even harder as you get older.

"Wanna go for a swim?" Jimmy asks suddenly. "It's the perfect night for it."

"Where do you swim?"

"There's a swimming hole just a little ways downriver. And there's cliff jumping for the really brave."

I don't answer. I'm too busy watching three girls walking along the sidewalk, wearing very short skirts and skintight tops. Their breasts bounce with each step.

"We can go back to Abigail's and grab shorts," he says. He's silent for a second. "Or we could skinny-dip."

"Skinny-dip?"

"Never mind. When you're ready."

"Let's just drive around some more."

In Unity, we swam fully clothed. I'm not ready to wear shorts, and I don't like the sound of "skinny-dipping," whatever that is.

"What do you want to take in college?" I ask Jimmy.

"I'm thinking of social work, but that's about seven years of university. I will have worn out my welcome at Abigail's by then."

"You'd be, like, twenty-eight or something. And still in school!" I laugh at the thought.

"Lots of people go to school when they're twenty-eight, Jon."

"They do?"

"Uh-huh. Sometimes it takes a while for a person to figure out what they're good at."

"What does a social worker do?"

"They try to make life better for people who don't have it so good. Like poor people, or people with disabilities. They also work for social justice."

"Social justice?"

"Sticking up for people's rights."

I think about that. "You're kind of doing social work already."

"By helping boys escape Unity?"

I nod.

"Maybe that's what made me think of it. Or maybe I already know what I'm good at."

Jimmy suddenly beeps his horn. Two guys on the sidewalk wave. "Jimmy!" one of them yells.

Jimmy pulls the pickup over to the curb and jumps out. He smacks hands with each of them. I notice that both are carrying beverage cans held together with plastic rings.

Jimmy talks to them for a few moments and then introduces me. The boys' names are Jared and Sam.

"New in town?" Jared asks.

"Yeah."

"Staying at Abigail's?"

I nod.

"Good lady." He turns to Jimmy. "We're going over to Alan's. Drink some beer. Play some frolf. You coming?"

Jimmy looks at me, eyebrows arched. I just shrug.

"Sure," Jimmy says. "Jump in the back."

The boys scramble into the truck bed, and Jimmy pulls back out onto the road.

"What's frolf?" I ask.

"Frisbee golf," Jimmy says. "You'll love it."

Minutes later we reach a small, neglected-looking house with old vehicles and furniture strewn about the front yard. The boys jump out of the truck and head around the side. Jimmy and I follow. The backyard is crowded with girls and guys, most about Jimmy's age. Sam and Jared stash their cans in a cooler of ice that's already full of cans and bottles. Sam offers us two of the already cooled ones.

"No thanks," I say, but Jimmy takes one and pops the cap off.

"I'm of age," he tells me.

The backyard isn't fenced and opens onto a large barren field. Hula-Hoops lie all over the field, and several kids take turns trying to land their Frisbees in the hoops. "It's not the official game," Jimmy tells me, "but it works for us."

He sees someone he knows and steps away, chatting with the guy about a work project. I stand back, feeling completely out of place and conspicuous in my pants and long-sleeved shirt. All the guys are wearing shorts and T-shirts—or even no shirt at all. Many have colored their hair in shocking tones of yellow or orange. Most have multiple tattoos, some large, covering whole arms or their entire backs. Others are small, like symbols. The Prophet would have freaked out if he saw these guys.

The girls are dressed much the same, but their clothes are tighter. Some wear sundresses that expose as much skin as wearing shorts and tight tops. They also have the full range of tattoos. I have to will myself not to stare.

"You must be one of Jimmy's roomies," a soft voice beside me says.

I turn and find myself looking down at a small girl with breasts the size of melons bursting out of her snug shirt. I try to focus on her eyes, but it's hard. I've never seen real breasts so close up. They look so much softer than the ones in the magazines that sometimes got smuggled into Unity.

"What's your name?" she asks, ignoring that I haven't responded. My mouth doesn't seem to be working.

"Jon," I say. "Without an *h*," I add stupidly.

"Nice to meet you, Jon-without-an-*h*," the girl says. "I'm Isobelle, with an *o*."

I suspect she's mocking me.

"Most people just call me Belle."

I can't think of anything to say to that either.

"Are you from Unity?"

I nod, wishing it wasn't so obvious.

"I just love hearing about Unity. It's so sweet and old-fashioned."

I'd like to set her straight on that, tell her there's nothing sweet about having every single part of your life controlled by the Prophet, or practicing a religion that doesn't allow for reasoning or questions, but before I can find the words, another girl hooks her arm through Isobelle's. "Hi," she says to me and then turns to Isobelle. "Beer pong has started. Let's go."

Isobelle gives me a big smile and a little wave. "See ya later, Jon."

I give her a feeble wave back and watch as the two girls take their places at one end of a picnic table lined with red plastic cups.

Jimmy finishes his beer and reaches into the cooler for another. He looks at me as he pulls a Frisbee out of a box. "Wanna play?"

"Sure."

Frisbee is something kids play in Unity. I can handle this.

He tosses me the Frisbee and, as we walk out to the playing field, gives me the rundown on how points are tallied. It takes me only three throws to get the Frisbee into the first Hula-Hoop. It takes Jimmy four. As we walk toward the starting base for the second hoop target, I become aware of how muggy and still the evening is. Jimmy has taken off his T-shirt. He takes long swigs from his can of beer.

By the time we get to the fifth hoop my entire shirt sticks to my body. I undo the top two buttons while Jimmy gets in position to throw the Frisbee. I leave the bottom four done up. My skin is deathly white compared to everyone else here, and I don't want my shirt flapping open to expose all of it.

I beat Jimmy at each of the hoops. A group of kids is waiting at the final target. I take my second shot and a cheer goes up. The Frisbee glides right into the center. It takes Jimmy two more tries to get his Frisbee in. There are high fives and pats on my back.

"Who's your ringer?" a guy asks Jimmy.

"He's on my team at the next tourney!" another guy shouts.

"Oh no. I found him," Jimmy says. "He's all mine."

Back in the yard, the crowd at the picnic table has become boisterous. Isobelle is still playing.

"Another beer?" Sam asks Jimmy.

"No thanks," he says. "I'm driving."

"Jon can drive."

He glances at me. I nod.

"Thanks," he says, "but we gotta go. It's a work night."

Isobelle catches my eye and jogs over. I can't help but watch her breasts bounce. "You're not leaving!" she says to me. Her cheeks are flushed, and her eyes glassy. "We didn't get a chance to talk!"

I glance at Jimmy for help.

"Yep, I'm taking him home," he says. "But no worries—
you'll be seeing him around."

"It was sooo nice meeting you, Jon-without-an-*h*," she
slurs. She throws her arms around me. I just stand there,
arms at my sides, hoping she'll let me go but also enjoying the
press of those breasts against my chest.

Jimmy grabs my arm and pulls me away. "Sorry, Belle.
Gotta go," he says.

I give her another feeble wave and follow Jimmy around
the side of the house.

"I think she likes you," he says, grinning.

Four

"Abigail sure likes having you here. I saw her face last night when she came home and smelled dinner cooking."

Taviana and I are cleaning up the breakfast dishes. Everyone else has left for work or school.

"Yeah, well, not enough to let me stay," Taviana answers, closing the dishwasher door and pushing the Start button.

"What do you mean?"

"I have until Monday to find somewhere else to live."

I stare at her. "Are you kidding? How come?"

"House rule number one—finish school. I can't do that." She gives the counter one last wipe.

"Why not? Abigail said you could get help if you're behind."

"It's not that. School is easy enough for me. It's the other kids."

"What about them?"

"They'd make my life impossible."

I watch her sweep the floor. "But you're not even a polyg like the rest of us. How bad can it be?"

"Real bad," she says.

I try to remember what I know about Taviana. She'd only lived in Unity about a year and a half. It was unusual for a gentile to choose to live there, but an elder, Jacob, had brought her to town, saying she needed a safe place. Celeste's father had offered to take her in because Celeste's mom was sick and they needed extra help at their house.

The boys in Unity talk, and there were stories that Taviana was a runaway who'd lived on the streets of Highrock, the next town down the river from Springdale. There were whispers that she had made money by having sex with men. Somehow Jacob had met her and felt compelled to help. From what I could see, she'd made a big effort to conform, wearing the long dresses that our girls wear and pitching in with community work. With her shorter hair and more worldly appearance, though, she was never really one of us. I know Celeste liked her and was heartbroken when the Prophet decided she had to leave. The way I heard it, he was afraid the authorities would think she was being kept in Unity against her will, so he had her dropped off in Springdale. That was the day before I arrived. I was able to get word to Jimmy that she was here. He located her wandering the streets and brought her to Abigail's.

"The kids here know about the stuff I used to do," Taviana says.

I decide not to ask about that. "Where will you go?"

"No idea. But I guess I'd better start thinking about it. I've been hoping Abigail would change her mind."

"If you helped out enough."

"Yeah."

I spend the entire day watching TV. Though the novelty is already wearing off, it helps me ignore the questions plaguing me: What has happened to Celeste? To my parents?

They will have realized by now that I'm gone. They'll be trying to keep it to themselves, as my running off will cast shame on my father. Fathers are supposed to have control over their children. When they don't, the Prophet can rip their wives and families away from them, assign them to another man. I don't think that will happen to my father. He seems to have a special ranking in the priesthood. Why else would he have been assigned some of the prettiest girls in Unity as his wives?

My mother was one of them. I sink lower on the couch. As her firstborn, I always felt like I was her favorite. I'd often look up from playing in the yard and find her gazing at me, smiling. Sometimes she'd hand me a little treat—a small candy—when no one else was looking. I badly wanted to please her, yet there was so much competition for her attention. Trying to anticipate her needs, I'd pick up the babies and rock them when they cried or bring her fresh carrots from the garden. When she was nursing one of my little brothers or sisters, I'd snuggle up beside her on the couch, and she'd pull me in close and quietly sing to me.

A mighty fortress is our Lord
A tower of strength ne'er failing
How measureless, how strong our Lord
I raise my song to thee.

I thought she had the most beautiful voice in the world.

Life wasn't all bad at home. In fact, it was pretty good a lot of the time. We'd go on camping trips, with a tent for each mom and her kids. My father and brothers and I often fished for rainbow trout at the lake on summer evenings. We'd go on long road trips to conferences where people of our faith from all over the country would gather to meet and socialize. In the car, we made up all kinds of games and pranks to amuse ourselves.

And cousins! There were enough for full soccer games on Sunday afternoons. I can't believe that I'll never see any of them again. Maybe I should have turned a blind eye to the discrepancies in our religion—what Jimmy calls hypocrisies. Then I'd still be part of my family. That counts for a lot.

Matthew and Selig stomp into the house. I shut off the TV. Matthew gives me a puzzled look. "You okay, Jon?"

I can only shrug. The thoughts of my family and Celeste have settled over me, pressing me down. My body feels like dead weight.

I even miss my chores. They gave me something useful to do to pass the time.

"Why don't we shoot a few baskets?" Matthew asks gently. He calls out to Selig. "Come play Around the World with us."

"Around the World?" I ask.

"Basketball for three players. We'll show you."

"Good news," Jimmy says, passing me a plate of lasagna. "My supervisor says we can go out to the job site on Saturday and take whatever scrap lumber we need for your planter boxes. He'll also find us some leftover paint."

"Cool." I try to muster up enthusiasm as I spear a cherry tomato from my salad. Building the planters doesn't have the same appeal tonight.

"You also have a meeting with the high school counselor next Monday," Abigail says. "She's going to run you through some tests, see where you'll fit in."

"They're not so bad," Matthew says, reading my face. "I took them too."

"I thought they were bad," Selig says. Matthew kicks him under the table.

"And what about you?" Abigail turns to Taviana. "Have you sorted anything out?"

Taviana shakes her head but doesn't look up. Everyone else grows quiet and focuses on their food too.

Taviana opens the bag of potato chips and hands it to me. "Salt and vinegar," she says. "C'mon. Try one."

I slide a chip onto my tongue and am assaulted by the strong flavor. "Yuck!"

Taviana laughs. "Maybe you'll like the plain ones better."

We've taken the bus into the town center so Taviana can use the library's computer to search for jobs and places to rent. I'm looking forward to going to the library to learn more about computers.

As soon as we walk through the door, the woman at the desk calls Taviana over. "Your card is ready," she says.

"All right! Now I'm going to read every single book in this place."

I look around, amazed at the rows and rows of shelves, stacked from top to bottom with books. Is Taviana serious?

She introduces me to the librarian, Audrey. "Would you like a library card too?" Audrey asks.

Taviana answers for me. "Yes, he would."

Audrey hands me a sheet of paper and tells me to fill in the information. Just basic stuff, like my name and birthdate. Taviana supplies me with Abigail's phone number and address.

"It will take a couple of days to process," Audrey says when I hand her the completed sheet. "You should have a card by early next week, if not sooner."

Taviana shows me around the library.

"Are there books on cars?" I ask.

She leads me to a shelf. "Voila!"

I read the titles on the book spines. *Off-Road Giants! American Auto Legends. Fix It! Automotive Wiring.* I choose a couple of books from the shelf and leaf through them.

Time disappears as I flip through the pages. There are lots of glossy photos. I read small sections, but slowly. I had no idea there was so much a person could learn from a book. I wish I could read faster. Everything I know about cars I learned from watching my father work on them, but there is so much more to know.

My eyes burn. I'm not used to so much reading. I return the books to the shelf and wander over to where Taviana sits at a screen.

"This is a computer," she tells me.

"I know that." I've seen them, but I've never used one. "What's so great about them anyway?"

"The Internet. Name something you want to learn about."

I think for a second. "Inuksuk."

Taviana positions me in front of the computer beside hers. "Type it in," she says.

"How do you spell it?"

As she tells me the letters, I push down on the keys, using one finger.

"Now push the Enter key."

A bunch of pictures of inuksuit suddenly appear on the screen. Taviana shows me how to use the mouse, as she calls it, to click on links.

"Look at them all! This is amazing. I wish I could show Celeste."

"You can find a lot of cool stuff on the Internet," Taviana says. She adds, "Except a job in Springdale, unfortunately."

"Are there books on inuksuk too?"

"Yep. The Internet can also help with that."

She shows me how to search the library catalog. It tells me where the books are shelved. Taviana takes me to the correct area.

"Choose two," she says. "I'll take them out on my card. When you get your own card, you can take out as many as you want."

It takes a few minutes to decide, but eventually I select a couple. Taviana has a stack of paperback novels to borrow. We take them all to the librarian.

"Do you know anyone who is looking for a summer job?" Audrey asks as she waves our books under some kind of scanner.

"Doing what kind of work?" Taviana asks.

"Mostly shelving returned material," she says. "We need someone to cover for staff on summer holidays. But we also need some enthusiastic people to help run the children's summer reading programs."

Taviana glances at me.

"Go on," I tell her.

"How do I apply?" she asks.

While Taviana fills out the application form, I flip through the pages of my books.

"We'll call you when we start interviewing," Audrey says. "Which should be the middle of next week."

Taviana's face crumples.

"Is something the matter?"

"No, not really. I'd just hoped to hear sooner."

"We have to go through the proper procedures," Audrey says. "But I'm sure you have a very good chance at the job."

"Thanks," Taviana says. "I hope so."

Outside the library, Taviana drops onto a bench. "I have to leave Abigail's in a couple of days," she says. "I won't be at the phone number I put on my application."

"Maybe Abigail will give you an extension."

"Maybe. But maybe not."

★　★　★

I leaf through my books while we wait at the bus stop.

Taviana jumps up suddenly. "I need to get something," she says.

"Are you okay?"

"I just need to run to the hardware store over there. I'll be right back."

I watch, puzzled, as she dashes across the street. Minutes later she's running back toward me. "Jon! Celeste is at the hospital. Right now!"

"What's the matter?" I leap to my feet.

"It's her mother. She's not well. Celeste is in town visiting her. I just met one of her other mothers in the store. I saw her go in with Celeste's father."

My heart is pounding.

"We can go over there right now. You can see her."

"Which way is it?"

Clasping our books, we run down the street and around a corner. Taviana points to a tower at the end of the block. "I'll go up to see them. And then I'll try to talk to Celeste alone. I'll tell her you're waiting in the front lobby. Wait by the entrance, and keep a lookout for her father. When Celeste finds you, you need to get out of the lobby as fast as you can so that when her father returns, he won't see you."

"Where should we go?"

"You'll figure something out." Taviana stops running and pulls on my arm, forcing me to stop too. "And Jon, there's something you need to know."

"What?"

Taviana frowns. "Celeste is getting married. On Sunday."

It's like someone has kicked me in the gut.

"And there's one more thing," Taviana says quietly.

I bend over at the waist, trying to suck in air, relieve the spasms.

"She's marrying your father."

At first the words don't register. But when they do, I feel such a swell of despair that I can only cover my face with my hands and turn away. "No," I moan.

I feel Taviana's hand on my back. "You okay?" she asks.

I bob my head, but it's a lie.

Five

Air-conditioning chills the hospital lobby, but that's not why I'm trembling. The minutes slowly tick by. What if Celeste can't sneak away? What if we're too late, and her father is already heading back to the hospital? What if—

The door to the stairwell bursts open, and there she is. Long blond braid. Pale blue eyes. Dark lashes. Floor-length Unity dress. An angel. She sees me and goes still. We stare at each other, and then suddenly she flies across the lobby and into my arms. I can't hold back the tears any longer and start to sob. She pulls away and looks at me. "Are you okay?"

I wipe my nose with my sleeve, wishing she hadn't seen me like this. "Yeah."

"We need to get out of here," she says, glancing at the door. "My father's due back any minute."

I look around the lobby and see a sign. *Visitors Waiting Area.* Grabbing her hand, I pull her into the small room and shut the door behind us. We wrap our arms around each other again, and for a moment I forget everything except the feel of her body pressed against mine, the smell of her skin, the beating of our hearts together.

When we finally pull apart we sit side by side on the vinyl couch, our hands clasped. "I never thought I'd see you again," she says. "This is such a shock."

"I know. I've missed you so much." I lean in and press my lips to hers. She responds, and nothing else matters.

The door bangs open. We jump apart, but it's just a woman with a small child. Seeing us, she pulls her child back out through the door.

"Celeste," I say. "Don't go back to Unity." I grip her hands harder. "Stay here with Taviana and me. We've found a nice lady who lets us live in her home as long as we go to school. You can come with us. We'll all be together."

Celeste sits back as she digests this. Her hands are shaking—or maybe it's my hands, holding hers, that are shaking.

"My father..." she says.

She doesn't have to finish the sentence. His fury will be frightening, and he may lose his priesthood if his daughter escapes. "I know. It's hard. But you have to be strong, Celeste. This is your life. Remember all those things we talked about by the river? How some things in The Movement just don't add up? Well, you being assigned to my father is one of those things. It's not divine revelation. Don't you see? It's punishment, pure and simple. They want to punish both of us."

. "I know, but my mother—she's so sick. I'm scared for her."

She paces the room, tormented. Occasionally she looks at me, then quickly looks away. She always said she could never leave, that she had no skills, no education. She figured she couldn't survive outside Unity.

But now things are different. She's been assigned to a husband. My father! Isn't that enough to give her the courage? And she'd have a home at Abigail's, which we didn't know about before. And she could go to school.

She sits beside me again, crying. I pull her close, and we rock back and forth, back and forth. I never want to let her go.

Eventually she pulls herself away. I look into her face. She won't meet my eyes.

My body deflates, a balloon releasing its air.

When she stands up, I clasp my hands in my lap. I can't look at her.

I hear her walk across the room and open the door. "I love you, Jon," she says, her soft voice shaky.

The door closes behind her.

"C'mon, Jon. It's garden-building weekend." Jimmy stands in the doorway to my bedroom.

"No. It's the day before Celeste's wedding day," I moan. The blankets on my bed are a rumpled mess, evidence of my fitful sleep. I find the edge of the sheet and pull it over my head.

I stared Satan down, and now I'm being punished. The Prophet can reach me even out here. All night I kept visualizing my father in Celeste's bed, his rough hands groping those places that I've been longing to stroke and explore. It makes me sick to think about it, yet I can't make the images go away.

"My supervisor is meeting us in one hour," Jimmy says. "He's going to unlock the fencing around the site so we can get the lumber. He knows you need work, so it's a good chance to meet him."

I can only groan.

"It'll help take your mind off things," Jimmy says more gently.

When Taviana and I returned to the house yesterday afternoon, I headed straight to my room and haven't been out since. Taviana must have filled the others in on what happened, because one by one they came to my door, offering sympathy and suggesting activities to take my mind off Celeste, but I only wanted to be left alone. Taviana brought me a plate of supper, but it still sits on the chest of drawers, untouched. I felt too sick to eat.

"We're leaving in twenty minutes," Jimmy tells me. "Tavi made muffins. You can grab a couple for the road."

Remembering Taviana's muffins from the night I arrived is just enough encouragement to help me haul myself out of bed and take a quick shower.

On my way out, Abigail hands me a lunch bag filled with warm muffins and juice boxes. "I can taste those homegrown veggies already," she says, her eyes filled with compassion as she steers me out the door.

At the construction site, Jimmy's supervisor, Alex, looks me over as he unlocks the chain-link fence. "I hear you're building yourself a garden," he says.

"Yes, sir, that's the plan."

"Jimmy tells me you've done some construction work in the past."

"I've been in construction full-time since I was fourteen."

"Is that so? Then you must know a thing or two."

"Yes, sir. I think I do."

Alex leads us over to a pile of scrap lumber at the edge of the site. His back is stooped, and when he shook my hand, I noticed how rough and gnarly his was, but his blue eyes are kind.

Like the librarian and the truck driver, Alex seems to be another good and honest gentile. How did the Prophet manage to convince us that they were all evil? It's hard to believe that the people of The Movement are the only ones that will go to heaven.

Alex helps us choose the best of the cedar planks and then watches us as we load them into Jimmy's pickup. He hands me a bag of timber screws. "You'll need these."

"Thank you. I will."

"I don't usually hire boys as young as you," he tells me. "But if you invite me over to see your garden, and I like your handiwork, I'll consider hiring you on for the summer. You seem like a good kid."

On the way back to Abigail's we stop at the nursery to buy soil and seeds. We argue for a long time about which vegetables to grow.

"I hate parsnips," Jimmy says. "I think we ate them every day when I was growing up."

I remove the envelope of zucchini seeds that he tossed in our cart and place it back on the display. "Bor-ing."

Jon snatches it. "But versatile. And easy to grow. We can make soup, muffins or stir-fry with zucchini."

I think of Taviana's muffins and stop arguing.

Eventually we choose beans, peppers, carrots, radishes (because Jimmy loves them), spinach and zucchini. We add small tomato plants to the cart and decide that if there's any room leftover in the garden we'll come back for onions and kale. We choose the largest and cheapest bags of soil that we can find, and we also grab a couple of bags of pea gravel for lining the bottoms of the planters.

The total comes to $145.

"Oh," I say to the cashier. "I only have one hundred dollars. I'll have to take some of it back."

Jimmy takes his wallet out of his pocket and pulls out forty-five dollars. "You can owe me," he says.

The four of us boys spend the afternoon building the raised garden boxes. We build them to run north to south and take full advantage of the sun. The hardest part is digging the trenches, but after that the work is easier. We stake the corners, then level and square up the first course of the cedar. I insist on being the one to screw the sides together, so Alex can see that I really do know what I'm doing. When we're finished there's lots of lumber left over, so we build a compost bin in the back corner of the yard. That complete, I add the pea gravel to the planters and fill them with soil. All that is left to do is plant the seeds.

The other boys have grown weary of working and are shooting baskets. Abigail left a pitcher of fresh lemonade and tuna-salad sandwiches on the small patio table for us. I take a sandwich and the seed envelopes and sit on the bottom step, intending to read the planting directions. But now that I've stopped working, my mind returns to Celeste. It's midafternoon. By this time tomorrow she'll likely be married. The families will be hosting a celebration dinner. Even though it's clear to both Celeste and me that this union has nothing to do with God's will, the priesthood will have to pretend that it does. All my family will be there. Everyone except me—the one Nielsson who actually loves Celeste. But, of course, love has nothing to do with marriage.

I think about my mom, who is Dad's second wife. How does she feel about welcoming yet another wife into the home? If she knows it was Celeste I was secretly meeting, she may be very angry with her.

Taviana comes out of the house and sits beside me. "Nice job," she says, looking at the planters.

"Thanks."

She leans her shoulder into mine. "You okay?"

I pretend to be really interested in reading the planting instructions on the radish envelope, but I can't see the words through my tear-filled eyes.

"At least your father is kind," she says. "And Celeste no longer belongs to her own father, who's so harsh."

I throw the seed packages to the ground, pull off my cap and rub my sweaty scalp. "Celeste shouldn't *belong* to anyone. Jimmy's right—those girls are brainwashed. It's bullshit! There are no divine messages. God doesn't tell the Prophet which girls should be assigned to which men. The select few from the priesthood just keep filling their homes with girls and calling them wives. It's fucked."

I can feel Taviana staring at me, shocked at my rant.

"She should have come with me," I add quietly. "She had her chance."

Abigail must have been standing behind the screen of the back door, listening. She steps outside, sits on the step above us and lightly rests a hand on my shoulder. "You know first-hand, Jon, how hard it is to even consider leaving your family when it's been the center of your universe."

"But I did it. And so did you."

"Yeah, I did. But not a day goes by that I don't wonder if I'd be happier if I'd stayed. I could have all my kids with me."

Taviana and I turn around, surprised.

I've never given any thought to *Abigail's* happiness.

"I know I did the right thing," she continues, "and I set a good example for my kids. I've shown them that they do have a choice. But leaving them behind? That was…" She shakes her head.

"Celeste didn't have to leave kids behind," I argue.

"No, but she would have had to leave everything else she knows. Facing the unknown is like jumping off a cliff without a parachute and with no idea of where you're going to land."

"We all did it," I say, including the other boys with my glance.

"Yeah, but many of you would have had to leave anyway, if you ever wanted to have a wife and family. You know there's not enough girls to go around."

Even I can do that simple math. It's one of the first things about our faith that led me to begin questioning it.

Abigail squeezes my shoulder and goes back into the house.

"Do you want some help with the planting?" Taviana asks.

"Thanks." I pick up the seed envelopes. "That would be great."

On Sunday morning, Taviana, the boys and I attend Abigail's church. I'm shocked at the informality. The building itself is not a church, just a hall with rows of chairs, and aside from a few old people in hats and jackets, I'm the only one dressed properly for a Sunday service. A woman leads us through a hymn and words of welcome. At first I can't figure out where the priest is, but then I realize she's the priest. A woman!

There's laughter during the service, and God is only referred to a few times, and when He is, it's in passing, without much reverence. There's no sermon. The priest just tells a story, weaving in Jesus's lessons about compassion. I found services boring in Unity, but I'm not sure what I think about this one. Have I betrayed God by coming here? Does He still love me?

★ ★ ★

"Isn't Sunday supposed to be a day of rest for your people?" Taviana asks after lunch. I'm back in the yard, sanding the top of the fence.

I glance up and see from the look on her face that she's teasing.

"Whatever."

"Why don't you come to the library with me? I need to check the computer for job postings, but then we can go to the park and chill. It will take your mind off things."

"Things." She means Celeste's wedding. "Do you think my card will be ready?"

"Might be."

"I guess the fence can wait until tomorrow."

Jimmy gives us a lift and drops us off at the library.

"Your card's ready, Jon," Audrey calls out as soon as we walk in. She flips through a small stack and hands it to me.

"How many books can I borrow?"

"As many as you want. You just have to return them before the due date or you'll be fined for each day that they're late."

I head straight to the books about inuksuk and the Arctic cultures that build them. I choose five. I'm tempted to get some books on cars too, but I decide to come back for those another day. When I return to the desk, Taviana's in deep conversation with Audrey. She's telling her about her situation, and how she's refused to go back to school because she knows the kids will torment her.

"Do you have a computer?" Audrey asks.

"No. Why?"

"You can take courses online."

"Oh!" Taviana's eyes light up. "Could I do them on the library computers?"

"I don't see why not. I'll look into it for you on my lunch break and call you at home."

"Actually," Taviana says, "we're going to the park for the afternoon. We'll stop in on our way back. Maybe Jon can leave his stack of books here so he doesn't have to carry them."

"Perfect. And I'll let you know then."

I take one book with me and leave the rest.

The park is crowded with families having picnics and enjoying the warm spring day. Aside from the way everyone is dressed, it doesn't look too different from what you'd see on a Sunday in Unity—extended families visiting, sharing food, kicking soccer balls, throwing Frisbees.

"Let's go up the river a ways," Taviana suggests.

As we pick our way along the stony beach, I see that Craig has been adding to his rock balances. I study each one, tempted to touch them to see how sturdy they are, but I resist. I wouldn't want them to tumble down.

When I turn around, Taviana has stripped down to just a couple of scraps of material. They barely cover her female parts. I avert my eyes, but I feel my skin burn.

"Get over it, Jon," she says. "This is what girls outside Unity wear to the beach." She takes two towels out of her bag. "Want to stretch out on that flat rock?" she asks, pointing to a boulder that rises out of the water.

"No, thanks. I think I'll sit in the shade and read."

"Suit yourself." She hands me a towel.

Taviana wades out into the water and climbs up on the large rock. She lays out her towel. I return to the shady spot under the tree where I spent my first afternoon in Springdale. I look up now and again and watch as Taviana climbs off the rock to splash in the water, keeping cool. I'm tempted to put my feet in, but I resist. Instead I read about Inuit culture and become completely absorbed.

Apparently no trees grow in the north, so houses can't be built from wood unless it's brought in. At one time, in the winter, Inuit lived in round houses made from blocks of ice, called igloos. In the summer they lived in tentlike huts made of animal skins stretched over a frame.

I'd love to share this stuff with Celeste. She'd be so amazed.

I don't know how much time passes, but eventually Taviana plunks herself down beside me under the trees. She's pulled her clothes back on over her bathing suit. "Ready to go?"

"Let's build an inuksuk first," I suggest.

"You don't think there's enough around here?" she asks, scanning the beach.

"There's always room for another."

Taviana sighs.

"What?"

"You're going to have to get over her eventually."

I ignore her and start looking for rocks that will make good legs.

★   ★   ★

Audrey grins when we push open the library door. "Good news," she says.

"I can use the library computers?" Taviana asks. "To complete high school?"

"You sure can," Audrey says. "And I've printed off all the information you'll need to register." She gives Taviana a thick envelope.

"Thank you!"

"There's just one small drawback," Audrey says.

"What's that?"

"The courses aren't cheap. Is that going to be a problem?"

"Maybe." Taviana frowns.

"Well, read over the information. Hopefully, you can make it work."

"Hopefully. All the more reason for me to get that job here."

The librarian holds up her hands. Her fingers are crossed for luck.

Back at the house, Abigail reads over the information while Taviana looks on nervously. "Well," Abigail says. "You really can do high school online."

"Then you'd consider me enrolled in school?" Taviana asks.

Abigail leans back in her chair. "Yes, I would," she says. "But Taviana, I can't afford these rates."

"Then I'll just have to figure out a way to pay for them myself. I'll get two jobs if I have to."

"You could apply for a student loan," Matthew suggests.

"I plan to work this summer," Selig says. "After I pay Abigail what I owe her, I'll give you what I don't need."

"You would, Selig?" Taviana's eyes shine with tears.

He nods.

"And if I grow more vegetables than we need," I say, "maybe we could sell them at the farmers' market." We passed the makeshift stalls on the way to the park today.

"I'll sell them for you," Jimmy says.

Taviana wipes her eyes and smiles. We all look at Abigail.

"Well, Tavi," she says, "it sounds like everyone's eager to help you. Between us, hopefully, we can find the money. I admit, it's nice to have another female in the house."

Taviana gives Abigail a long hug. She then hugs each of us. I hug her back awkwardly. Selig and Matthew look awkward too. Jimmy has no trouble with it.

"Well, this family has an official second female member," Abigail says. "And that calls for a celebration dinner. You boys haul out the old barbecue and clean it, and Tavi and I will go out and buy the ingredients for a special meal. How about it?"

The boys stampede into the backyard. I lag behind. I'm happy that Taviana has sorted out her schooling, but the word *celebration* reminds me of the one that took place in Unity today.

I join the boys in the backyard and try not to think of Celeste, my father's sixth wife.

Six

On Monday morning I walk to Springdale High with Matthew and Selig. The hallways are loud with kids grabbing books from their lockers and calling out to their friends. A buzzer sounds. Lockers bang shut, and everyone jostles each other as they head to their classes. The stretch of warm weather has continued, and the kids are dressed much like they were at the park, in shorts and T-shirts.

I will myself not to stare at the girls with their long, exposed legs and jiggling breasts and keep my eyes glued to Matthew's back as he leads me through the maze of halls to the school office. Aside from the way everyone is dressed, the other thing that strikes me is how young the students are. Many look to be only thirteen or fourteen.

Matthew shows me to the office. "Just tell the school secretary that you're here to see Mrs. Kennedy. She'll show you where to go. I've got to run to history class. Good luck, Jon."

I must look panicked, because he squeezes my arm and says, "It'll be fine."

It's far quieter in the office than in the hallways. Two women sit at desks, and two men talk beside a water cooler. I'm surprised that the men are wearing shorts, but, in general, the adults are dressed more modestly than the teenagers. That should make it easier to concentrate on the exams I'm about to take.

The school secretary leads me to a chair outside an office down the hall. "Wait here," she says.

The adults who walk past all say hello. I'm sure it's clear to everyone that I'm a polyg. I put on a clean shirt this morning, but the armpits are wet with sweat. I lay awake most of the night, worrying about the exams.

Finally the door opens and Mrs. Kennedy invites me into her office. She's about my mom's age, but tiny, birdlike, with short spiked hair. Her desk is cluttered with file folders. I take the chair across from her. She looks tired but not unkind.

"Abigail tells me you're from Unity," she says.

I nod.

"How long have you been in Springdale?"

"One week."

"And how are you adjusting?"

"Fine, I think."

"That's good. I'm sure Matthew and Selig have made you feel welcome."

"They have."

"Good. Nice boys, those two." She studies me, but I can't read her face. "When did you last attend school?"

"I left when I was fourteen."

"And you're seventeen now?"

I nod.

She sighs and picks up a pen. Her thumb presses the button on the end. Click. Click. Click. "From what I know about your school in Unity, the emphasis is on religious studies," she says. "I don't mean to sound critical, but it seems that the basics are just barely covered. There is no instruction in history, science or current events." Click. Click. "And literature and the arts are frowned upon, right?"

She waits for me to correct her, but what is there to say? I barely know what literature is. Or science. I don't say anything.

"Have you heard of global warming, Jon?"

I shake my head.

"How about Donald Trump. Do you know who he is?"

"I've heard the name."

"What about Adolf Hitler?"

"What about him?"

"Do you know who he is? What he did?"

"No."

"Have you used computers?"

"Yes. At the library. In Springdale." I don't tell her that it was only once.

She looks out the window. Click. Click.

"I know how to frame a house," I say, feeling the need to defend myself.

She gives me a warm smile. Her face instantly looks ten years younger. "I bet you do. And I bet there's no other student in this school who could do that."

"Maybe Matthew and Selig."

"Right. Except for them. And I'm sure you have a whole lot of other skills that you don't learn in school. I'm not trying to make you feel bad about the gaps in your education. I'm just trying to decide how best to bring you up to speed." She lays the pen down and folds her hands behind her head. "Jon, what kind of a career would you like when you finish school?"

Aside from Craig, the boy on the beach, no one has ever asked me that. I have no answer. I don't even know what careers there are to choose from.

"Do you think you'd like to go to college or trade school?"

"Yeah, I would."

"You would?" She is pleasantly surprised.

"My friend Jimmy wants to go to college to become a social worker. That sounds cool. I'd like to help people too." Truthfully, I've never given it much thought, but I feel I need to say something.

"I'm sure you'd be a wonderful social worker." She looks pleased with this answer. "The trade schools offer careers that you already have a background in. You could be an electrician or a cabinet maker." She frowns. "But no matter what, you need a high school diploma. Jon, I had planned to give you the ninth-grade final exams in each subject, but I don't think there's any point. If you haven't been taught the subjects, you're not going to know the answers. It doesn't mean you're not smart—it just means you haven't been given the information. I don't want to set you up for failure. I think I made a mistake putting the other boys through that."

Relief surges through me.

"What I am thinking is that we should find a tutor to work with you over the summer. The tutor would instruct you in every subject, try to get you caught up."

"A tutor?"

"A teacher who works one-on-one with you."

"Book learning." The Prophet used to sneer at the term.

"Right."

"Would I have to pay this tutor?"

"Yes, you would."

"I don't have any money." I slump in my chair.

"But you do intend to work this summer?"

I nod.

"Well then, I could send you home with the textbooks to get you started. Once you have your first paycheck, you could call the tutor and set up a schedule. Selig and Matthew might even want to share the same tutor."

I hadn't intended to use my earnings for school, but if it helps me get caught up...

"Are you willing to do schoolwork each night this summer, Jon?"

I nod, though I've also warmed to the idea of driving around with Jimmy, meeting his friends, playing frolf.

"Okay. I'll call around and find a tutor who works over the summer. If you come back tomorrow, I'll have a package of tenth-grade materials ready for you. You will likely need instruction in ninth-grade math as well. I'd also like you to watch the news and read the newspaper each day, to get familiar with current events. And read books. The stronger your reading becomes, the easier it will be for you to get through the course material."

"I already have a library card," I say. I feel like I'm a little kid again, trying to please my mom.

"That's great, Jon." Mrs. Kennedy's smile is warm. "I can tell that you're the kind of student who will work hard to overcome the gaps in your education. In the fall, you'll start eleventh grade. But it's going to be a stretch to get you caught up to the end of tenth grade in just one summer."

"Eleventh grade?"

"That's what I'm recommending."

"But I'll be way older than the other kids."

"Just by a year or two. And that's okay."

It doesn't feel okay to me. "I know a girl who is doing high school by using the Internet. Maybe I should do that."

Mrs. Kennedy considers this for a moment. "I don't think that would be a good option for you. Online courses don't assume you have gaps in your knowledge. Here, the teachers will be aware of your background."

"They'll know I'm a stupid polyg," I mutter.

"Pardon me?"

"Nothing."

She leans forward. "With the right attitude and hard work, you'll be graduating in a couple of years. By then, you just might know what you'd like to do with your future."

★ ★ ★

After carefully watering my new garden boxes, I close the curtains in the living room and hunker down in front of the TV. I know I could be practicing my reading, but my head hurts just thinking about all the reading I'll be doing over the next few months.

Taviana bustles in through the door. There's a sheen of sweat across her forehead, and her cheeks are flushed.

"Where have you been?" I ask.

"Out for a jog. I figure I'd better get in shape before I start my online classes." She pinches the skin on her waist. "I'm getting soft, and there might not be much time for exercising once I get a job and start studying."

I roll my eyes. There's nothing soft about her. The Prophet says that hard work is all a person needs to do to stay strong. I tend to agree with him on that. All this jogging to nowhere seems like a waste of energy.

"I'll shoot some baskets with you," Taviana says.

"No thanks. I'm good." My eyes return to the TV.

She plunks herself down beside me on the couch. The show has resumed. "Jerry Springer? Really, Jon? There's nothing better on than this?"

"I have to find out who the father of Chantal's baby is,"

I tell her. "I think it's that jerk Spade. Boris has a good alibi, and Spencer looks too decent."

"Jon, get a grip." Taviana picks up the remote control and shuts off the TV.

"Hey, I was watching that!" I try to grab the remote, but she holds it behind her back. I'm tempted to reach around her and tussle to get it, like she and Selig did with the book, but I don't feel right wrestling with a girl.

"I need to tell you something." Taviana scuttles away from me on the couch.

"What?"

"There's a lot of good stuff on TV, but don't make a habit of watching this kind of crap. It's addictive."

"How do you know?"

"My mother watched this stuff all the time, and then she began behaving like those people."

"I'm not going to behave like Spade."

"You say that now. This stuff drags you down. Trust me. Soon you'll find that those people seem normal to you. Find something inspiring to watch, or read a book."

"Those people will never seem normal to me. I grew up in Unity, remember?" The truth is, I'm amazed at how badly these TV people behave. "Anyway, after today I'll be spending my whole summer reading. This may be my last chance to chill."

"What happened at school?"

"I didn't have to write the exams."

"Really?"

"Mrs. Kennedy said I'd just fail them. She's recommending a tutor for the summer, and then I'll start eleventh grade in the fall." I take a deep breath. "I'm too old to just be starting eleventh grade."

Taviana doesn't answer. I take her silence as agreement.

"I asked if I could do online courses like you, but she didn't recommend it."

As Taviana ponders that, I swipe back the remote and turn the TV on again.

We both stare at the show for a few minutes, but now I don't really care who Chantal's baby's father is. Taviana has ruined it for me.

I flick through the stations. I stop at one and put the remote down. "Homework," I tell her. "I'm supposed to watch the news."

"Okay," she says. "I'm going to have a shower, but if you want to work on your math skills, you can help me make a pie crust later."

"How will that help my math skills?"

"I'll let you do the measuring."

Just as Mrs. Kennedy directed, I bring two large bags with me when I return to the school. On her desk she now has a stack of textbooks, exercise books and papers stapled and paper-clipped together.

"I know. It's a little overwhelming at first," she says when she sees my face. "But you'll work through it."

She obviously doesn't know how slowly I read.

"I've also talked to a young man who is willing to tutor you. He's the son of a friend of mine, and he has some free time this summer. His phone number's here." She hands me a small yellow paper. I look at the name. *Craig*. Could it be the same guy I met by the river? The inuksuk guy?

I stuff the books and papers into my bags.

"I'm confident that you'll be successful, Jon," Mrs. Kennedy says. "You have a lot of ground to cover, but it will be worth it. Trust me."

Trust me.

Taviana said the same thing.

Jimmy drives away after dinner. I wonder if he's going to play some more frolf or go swimming. I'd really like to drive around town with him, listening to music, but instead I take a book out of my bag. I read the title: *Essential Biology*.

"What's biology?" I ask Matthew, who is doing math homework at the kitchen table. Selig has gone to the library to work on the computer. Taviana went with him to help with his project on the novel they're both reading.

"Science."

"Then why don't they just call it *Essential Science*?"

"Because there's different kinds of science."

I pull out a couple more textbooks. *Chemistry 10, Introduction to Physics.* "Like these?"

Matthew looks up from his math problem. "Yep."

I fan the pages. "How am I ever going to get through all this?"

Matthew sighs. "One page at a time."

"You're doing eleventh grade this year, right?"

He nods.

"And Selig is doing tenth?"

"Yeah. We're the same age, but he's only been here a few months. Mrs. Kennedy put him in tenth grade. He's not finding it easy. Neither of us is." He studies his pencil.

"Do you have tutors?"

"Peer tutors. Other kids at school. They get volunteer credit for it."

"Do you think you're going to pass everything?"

Matthew shrugs. "Hard to say. I'm trying. But Selig"— Matthew shakes his head—"is really struggling."

I look at his math homework. It almost seems like a foreign language. "Is it worth it?"

He returns to his math problem. "I hope so."

"Someone here to see you, Jon," Jimmy says. He's just come in from work. I'm in the kitchen, helping Taviana make hamburger patties for dinner.

"Who?"

"Alex. My boss. He's in the backyard, looking at your garden boxes."

I wash and dry my hands and follow Jimmy out the back door. There's Alex, walking around the garden, checking my handiwork. His truck is parked in the alley.

"Hi, Jon," he says when I join him. "I see you've already finished building your garden."

"Yeah. And we had enough wood left over for a compost box too."

He steps over to look at it.

"This is really good work, Jon. I can see your attention to detail even in this small project."

"Thank you. The guys all helped me."

"But Jon did most of it," Jimmy says. "We were just his gofers."

"I hope you'll share a few of your vegetables with me when they're grown," Alex says, smiling.

"Of course."

"I'm also hoping you'll start work on Monday. You'd be on the same crew as Jimmy."

"That'd be great!"

"I've got some half-full cans of fence paint in my truck," Alex says. "I heard that you also want to do some painting back here."

"The fence. I've begun sanding it already," I tell him. "Maybe I can get it done before I start work next week."

Abigail comes down the steps, and Jimmy introduces her to Alex.

"You're a lucky woman having these fine young men living under your roof," Alex says. He smiles at her.

She smiles back, and her face is transformed. No more bulldog. "Taviana is making burgers," she says. "Why don't you stay and have one with us?"

Alex removes his hat and runs his hands through his wisps of gray hair. "Well, I'm just coming off work. I'm not really dressed for dinner."

"It's just an informal barbecue," Abigail says. "No need to worry about how you're dressed."

"Well then, if that's the case, sure," he says. "And I can admire these fine garden boxes a little longer."

We sit in creaky lawn chairs to eat our burgers. Abigail has made fresh lemonade, and Taviana whipped up strawberry shortcake for dessert.

"This is the finest meal I've had in a long time," Alex says. He sits back in his chair, looking relaxed. Jimmy is helping Taviana in the kitchen, and Matthew and Selig are shooting baskets.

"It was just burgers," Abigail says, sitting beside him and looking just as relaxed. "But Taviana has real skills in the kitchen."

Alex asks Abigail about her job as a care aid in the nursing home. He probes into her decision to leave Unity and take in Lost Boys. She answers honestly. "Providing these boys with a place to live gives my life meaning," she says. "Not that working in the care home doesn't, but the boys help me feel connected to my own children, the ones I don't see anymore."

"I admire your courage," Alex says. "I'm sure you've paid a big price for your freedom."

Abigail's eyes fill with tears. "What about you?" she asks, changing the subject. "Do you have family?"

Alex is slow to answer. "I was married for thirty years. My wife died a year ago. Our boys moved away, preferring city life. They come to visit on holidays, and we keep in touch. They're good sons, but I sure miss them."

Selig and Matthew whoop as Selig sinks a three-pointer. The evening is warm, and the light is soft.

"Well, I guess I should call it a night," Alex says. "But I sure appreciate your hospitality, Abigail." He rises stiffly from his chair. "And I look forward to seeing you next Monday, Jon. I know you'll be a good addition to the crew."

He shakes my hand.

"Thanks for the paint," I say.

"You're welcome."

"You'll have to come back soon," Abigail says. "See if Jon paints as well as he builds."

"I will," Alex says.

As I unload the paint from his truck, he snags the basketball on a rebound and makes a jump shot. He's surprisingly agile. The ball sails through the hoop.

"Ha!" he says. "I haven't lost it after all."

Seven

Craig is reading in a corner of the coffee shop when I arrive with a heavy bag of textbooks. He looks up from his newspaper and smiles.

"So it is you!" he says.

"It's me." I return his smile.

I'm glad he remembers me. When I called him to make the appointment, I didn't mention that I thought we'd already met. He said he was happy Mrs. Kennedy had given me his number, because he needed the income. I'd asked Matthew and Selig to join me and share the costs, but they both turned down the offer. Craig agreed to let me pay him after I get my first paycheck.

"What do you want to drink?" he asks as I sit down in the chair across from him.

"Nothing, thanks."

"We're expected to buy something if we're going to work in here," he says quietly.

I notice the mug on the table in front of him. "I only have enough money for bus fare."

"No worries. I'll get you something. Do you drink coffee?"

I shake my head.

"A cola?"

"No." I never developed a taste for cola. The Prophet frowned upon any caffeinated drinks.

"How about hot chocolate?"

"That sounds good."

Craig hands me a five-dollar bill. "You order it, and I'll take a look through your textbooks."

When I give the girl at the counter the five-dollar bill, she gives me twenty-five cents in change. I look at the coin sitting in my hand. "Something wrong?" the girl asks. There's a large diamond stud poking out the side of her nose, and the tips of her hair have been dyed pink. I can tell she's sizing me up too, probably noting that I'm a polyg. It might be time to change my look a bit. Maybe a T-shirt wouldn't be so bad.

"No. Just thought I'd get back more change."

"The prices are on the board," she says, glancing up at the menu chalked onto the wall behind her.

"Yeah, I see them, but—"

"Plus tax." She looks at the person behind me. "Can I help you?"

Tax? I collect the mug, heaped with whipping cream. Back at the table, I push the coin across the table to Craig. "Sorry," I say. "That's all the change I got."

Craig doesn't answer. He's busy underlining titles on the recommended reading list. He grins when I sit back down. "Some of my favorite novels are on here," he says. "We're going to have fun. I've underlined the ones you should read first."

"Fun?"

"You don't like reading?"

"I've never done much reading," I admit, not wanting to bring up the Prophet's thoughts on books. "Though I did get a library card last week and took out some books on inuksuk and the Inuit culture."

"You did?" His face lights up.

I nod.

"We're going to get along just fine."

We spend an hour skimming the topics in the first unit in each of the textbooks, and Craig makes a list of the pages I should read and the problems I should try solving before we meet again in a week.

My brain feels sore from concentrating. Finally we pile the books and papers back into the bags. "I'll go by the library on my way home," I say. "I'll sign out one of those novels."

"Good on you," Craig says. "My work this summer is to get you through these courses, but my personal goal is to get you excited about books."

"I just hope I learn to read faster," I tell him as I hoist the heavy bags. "Otherwise I'll never get through all this."

Craig pats me on the back as we head out into the sunshine. "Yes you will."

I spend the rest of the afternoon sanding the fence. At dinner, Matthew and Selig discuss their applications for summer jobs and the high school softball game they're going to that evening. Jimmy is taking Taviana to meet his friends and play some frolf. They're celebrating Taviana's new job at the library. I'm invited to join both groups, but I'll never get through all my homework for Craig if I don't start it tonight.

After helping with the dishes, I take my library copy of *To Kill a Mockingbird* into the backyard, make myself comfortable in a lawn chair and turn to the first page.

I'm up early on Monday morning to water my garden before heading to work with Jimmy. The sky has clouded over, and the air temperature has dropped. It's a good day for framing houses.

Alex dropped by on Sunday with the excuse of bringing me an old pair of work boots and a carpenter tool belt. He arrived late in the afternoon, and I suspect he was actually looking for another dinner invitation, which he got. He could have given me the boots and belt this morning. As it turned out, he was able to inspect the newly repaired and painted fence, which, I admit, I'm proud of.

At the job site, a new neighborhood on the edge of town, Jimmy introduces me to the two other framers, Charlie and Ross.

Alex is overseeing a number of houses in the new subdivision, so he gives us our instructions and promises to return later.

It only takes a short time before I'm back in the rhythm of building, and I relax, glad to be doing something I know I'm good at. We measure, saw and hammer until midmorning, when Charlie calls for a coffee break. He and Ross pour coffee out of thermoses and light up cigarettes. Jimmy and I guzzle water from our bottles and dig out the cookies from our lunch bags.

"You've framed before," Charlie says, taking a long drag on his cigarette. I'm guessing both men are in their early thirties, older than Jimmy but younger than my father.

I nod, secretly glad that he's noticed. I'm a whole lot more comfortable doing this than reading textbooks.

"How long have you been out of Unity?" Ross asks. His arms are covered in tattoos, and he has a gold stud in one earlobe.

"Two weeks."

"Had any fun yet?" he asks, grinning.

"Ross," Charlie says. There's a warning tone in his voice.

"Just wondering if he's still pure," Ross says, blowing out a long stream of smoke.

Jimmy changes the subject. "I hear we're in for a long hot summer," he says. It's a lame comment, but he's trying to protect me from Ross's prying.

"That so?" Ross says, grinding his cigarette out with the toe of his boot. "Who'd you hear that from?"

"The meteorologist on the news."

I look at him. "Meteorologist?"

"Weatherman. Or woman, in this case."

"Speaking of women," Ross says, "how many wives does your father have, Jon? I've always fantasized about having a whole harem of them, like you guys do."

"Ross," Charlie warns again.

"It's okay," I tell him. I look directly at Ross. "He has five." Then I remember. "Make that six." I swallow hard and look away.

"My father had six too, last I heard," Jimmy says.

Ross reaches over and whips up the front of Jimmy's T-shirt.

"What are you doing?" Jimmy takes a step back and tucks in his shirt.

"Just wondering if you had six belly buttons. You know, one for each mother."

To my surprise, Jimmy laughs. "Good one."

Jimmy is so comfortable with his friends, with these co-workers and just generally with life outside Unity, that I often forget he was once a polyg too.

Alex's truck crunches on the gravel driveway. The older men screw the lids back onto their thermoses while Jimmy and I stash our lunch bags in the cooler.

Alex hobbles over to inspect our work. He pulls off his cap and scratches his head. "You got a lot done already this morning," he says, nodding. "Keep this up, and I might be able to set you loose early on Friday afternoon. With pay, of course."

The men grin, and Charlie takes up his hammer and starts pounding nails again. "C'mon, you guys," he says. "I'll buy the first round on Friday if we get off early."

★ ★ ★

When I water the garden after dinner I see a soft fringe of green where the radishes are sprouting. Very lightly I run my fingers over the green tops, pleased. Then I settle back at the kitchen table beside Selig and Matthew. There's an explosion of paper and books on the table.

"I really need a computer," Matthew grumbles after a few minutes of quiet studying. "It's too far to go to the library every time I need to look something up."

"She's working on it," Selig whispers, glancing at the door to the living room. We can hear the whir of Abigail's sewing machine. She's started taking in tailoring jobs to earn extra cash.

"We're already at a disadvantage, coming from Unity," Matthew complains, "and everyone else has computers at home."

The sewing machine grows quiet. We go back to studying.

"Any callbacks from your job applications?" Selig asks Matthew a few minutes later.

Matthew shakes his head. "You?"

"There's a dishwashing job, but it's minimum wage."

"Better than nothing," Matthew says.

"You don't want to work in construction?" I ask them, feeling guilty that I landed a job without even looking for one.

They both shake their heads. "Been there, done that," Matthew says.

"Never want to do it again," Selig agrees.

"You'd rather wash dishes?" I ask.

"At least there's girls working at the restaurant."

Matthew smiles and turns the page of his textbook. "Exactly."

★   ★   ★

When we break for lunch on Friday, Ross pulls something out of the pocket of his flannel work shirt. It looks like a cigarette, but with twisted ends. "Care to join us, boys?" he asks Jimmy and me. "Get the weekend started?"

"No thanks," Jimmy says, laying his tools down a little too firmly. "Come on, Jon."

"Relax, Jimmy," Ross says. "It's time to break the new kid in."

Jimmy doesn't respond. I don't say anything either. I follow him to his truck. We take our lunches out of the cooler and find a shady spot beside the framed house. Charlie has followed Ross to his pickup truck, and they're both sitting in the cab.

"What was that?" I ask Jimmy.

"A joint. Marijuana." He unwraps a sandwich and takes a huge bite.

I just look at him.

"They smoke it and get high."

"Oh." The Prophet has told us about the gentiles' drugs, which are worse even than books, according to him.

Jimmy shakes his head. "I don't care if they use it. I just wish they wouldn't smoke it at work. It slows them down."

"Do you think Alex still plans to let us quit early today?"

"Not if he knows those two are smoking pot on the job."

But when Alex comes by shortly after lunch, he doesn't realize Charlie and Ross have smoked the joint, or if he does he doesn't mention it. I don't know how he could miss the lingering skunk-like smell in the air. He hands out paychecks to the other three. I have to work another week before I get one. "You've made excellent progress this week," he tells us. "We're ahead of schedule. Jon, you're a great addition to the team. Go on home now, all of you, and have a good weekend."

Charlie packs up his tools. "He seems to be in an especially good mood this week," he comments after Alex has driven away. "Have you noticed?"

No one answers, but Jimmy looks at me and raises his brows.

"Don't forget—the first round is on me," Charlie says. "I'll meet you at the Black Bear Pub in twenty."

"Thanks, Charlie," Jimmy says, "but Jon's underage, and I have plans."

"Suit yourself."

On our way home Jimmy stops at the bank to deposit his paycheck and then runs into the drugstore. I sit back and close my eyes. My whole body aches from the week's work, but in a good way. I much prefer this kind of ache to the headache I get from reading textbooks each night.

Jimmy's grinning when he returns. He tosses a bag on the truck bench between us. As he backs out of the parking stall, I look into the bag. "Hair dye?"

"Yup."

"Who's dyeing their hair?"

"It's time for Matthew and Selig's initiation. They've both been here long enough."

"Initiation?"

"Yeah. Time to turn them into real gentile boys."

"What about you?"

"I did it too. When I first arrived."

I've noticed that lots of the kids in Springdale, boys and girls, color their hair. "How long do I have to wait to be initiated?"

Jimmy glances at me. "You want to dye your hair too?"

I think about it. The Prophet would explode into a billion pieces if a kid from Unity dyed his hair. "Yeah." I smile at him. "I think I do."

"Right on, Jon!"

At Abigail's I read for a while, finishing up the chapters that Craig assigned. When Matthew and Selig get home from school, the four of us shoot some baskets and then flop on the couch in front of the TV. Jimmy is in the chair, talking on his cell phone.

"What a week," Selig groans. "Three exams, and I bet I flunked every one of them."

Taviana comes in and squeezes onto the couch between Selig and Matthew. "I've got news," she says.

We all look at her. Jimmy ends his call.

"Abigail is going out for dinner with Alex tonight."

"I figured something was up," Jimmy says. "The guys at work noticed that Alex's been in a good mood all week."

"She says he's just reciprocating for his dinners here," Taviana says. "But I think it's a date."

I'd noticed that Abigail went straight to her room when she got home from work and shut her door firmly.

"Well, if she's going out, I'll buy pizza for the rest of us," Jimmy says. "It was payday today. And have I ever got a surprise for you boys." He points at Matthew and Selig, smiling.

Selig frowns. "What is it?"

"You'll have to wait and see."

Jimmy lets Alex into the house when he arrives. We all stare at him. Gone are the work clothes. His strands of hair are combed neatly into place, and he's wearing clean, pressed slacks and a dress shirt that's tucked in at the waist. The scent of his aftershave overpowers the fragrance of the flowers he's carrying.

"Hi, boys," he says, somewhat sheepishly. "Hello, Taviana."

And then we all do a double take as Abigail comes down the hall. She's in a flattering skirt and blouse, and her face looks different. I take a closer look and realize that she's wearing makeup. Her hair has been brushed out loose, with just a clip to hold it off her face. The effect is startling, and we all watch as she greets Alex and graciously accepts the flowers.

"Thank you, Alex," she says. "They're beautiful."

Taviana takes them from her and promises to put them in water. Then we all gather at the window and watch as Abigail takes Alex's arm to walk down the driveway. He opens his truck's passenger door for her and helps her to climb up.

"Go figure," Jimmy says.

"It's so sweet!" Taviana has her hand pressed against her chest. She has the same look on her face that I've seen on the women's faces in Unity when one of the girls is being married. The truck drives away, and Taviana picks up a book. "Let me know when the pizza arrives," she says. "I'll be reading in the backyard."

Jimmy orders pizza, then clicks off the TV and holds up the brown paper bag. "Are you ready for your surprise?" he asks Matthew and Selig.

They regard him suspiciously.

"I have your graduation presents."

"Graduation from what?" Selig asks, flopping back on the couch. "I'm never going to graduate from high school."

"Not school graduation. Graduation from your old way of life. You now wear short-sleeved shirts and shorts. You talk to girls. You've seen the light!" He laughs. "You two are now certifiable gentile guys." Jimmy dumps the contents of the bag onto the couch. He holds up the boxes. "Hair dye! We have Electric Banana and Neon Orange. What's your choice, Matthew?"

Matthew laughs. "Electric Banana!" He takes a box and studies the picture on the front.

"You want to be Neon Orange, Selig?" Jimmy asks.

"I don't know."

"How about you?" Jimmy asks me.

"Why not?"

Jimmy turns back to Selig. "We'll do those guys first, and then you can pick your favorite color. If you don't like either, I'll get you another one. Maybe blue?"

"What about you?" Selig asks him. "Aren't you going to dye yours?"

"Been there, done that. I'm now thinking of doing something…a little more permanent." He doesn't explain further. "Come on. Into the bathroom."

Although Selig is clearly not as excited about dyeing his hair as Matthew is, he follows us into the tiny room anyway.

Jimmy reads the directions on the box and then gets the mixing bowl out, along with the tube of dye and the paintbrush.

Taviana has come back into the house and stops abruptly as she walks past the bathroom door. She peers in. I'm sitting on the toilet, lid down, awaiting my turn, and Selig is on the edge of the tub. Jimmy and Matthew are at the sink. "What are you guys up to?" she asks.

"Dyeing Matthew's hair," Jimmy says, pulling on the latex gloves.

"Oh my god," she says. "You'll make a mess. Abigail will kill you."

"We'll be careful," Jimmy says.

"Have you ever done it before?" she asks.

"Well, no," Jimmy admits. "I had mine done at a salon."

"Hang on a sec," Taviana says and scurries away. When she returns, she's wearing an apron and carrying newspaper, rags and a pile of old towels. "Make sure you take off your shirts," she says. "Or you'll ruin them. And keep a rag handy to wipe your face. Trust me."

"You've done this before?" Jimmy asks.

"Yep. Now everyone out. I have to cover the floor and counters with newspaper."

The next thing we know, Taviana is wearing the latex gloves and applying the dye to Matthew's hair. He has an old towel around his bare shoulders and has taken Selig's place on the side of the tub. "You have to wait fifteen minutes while it does its thing, and then you wash it out," she says, pulling a flimsy shower cap over Matthew's head.

"Cool," Matthew says.

"Who's next?" Taviana asks.

"Jon is," Jimmy tells her.

"Shirt off, Jon," Taviana instructs.

"Just put a towel over my shoulders," I say.

Taviana stares at me. "You don't want to take your shirt off." It's a statement, not a question.

Matthew laughs, but gently. "Come on, Jon. This is a graduation ceremony, remember? Shirt off. You're no longer a polyg."

I meet Selig's eyes, and he shrugs and looks away.

I slowly unbutton my shirt and take it off. I catch a glimpse of my pale skin in the mirror.

"Toss it to Jimmy," Taviana instructs. "We don't want any random dye drips to wreck it."

I ball it up and throw it into the hall.

"Now that wasn't so hard, was it?" Taviana asks, wrapping a towel around my shoulder. "What color are you going?" She picks up the second box and reads the label. "Neon Orange. Cool." She begins the preparations.

No, I realize as she begins to paint my hair, it wasn't so hard, except that now Taviana is hovering over me, and I'm acutely aware of how close she is. I can even feel the heat radiating off her. The smell of her deodorant is fruity. My face is level with her chest as she works, and I don't want anything embarrassing to happen.

The doorbell rings. Jimmy and Selig hustle down the hall to get the pizza.

"Save some for us!" Matthew hollers after them.

"Okay, Matthew," Taviana says once she's finished with me. "You can either get in the shower and wash your hair, or lean over the sink and I'll wash it for you."

Matthew's eyes flick over to me and then back to Taviana. "I might as well shower," he says. "Protect the sink and counter from getting Electric Banana drips."

"I'll shower after you," I tell him. I'm not concerned about the counter and sink. I just don't know what might happen if

Taviana was leaning over me, washing my hair, pressing up to my bare torso.

I suspect that Matthew was thinking the exact same thing.

I'm eating pepperoni pizza in the kitchen, my hair covered with a shower cap, when Matthew comes strutting down the hall, fresh out of the shower. He's still bare-chested, and his hair is a ridiculously unnatural shade of yellow. He's used his fingers to spike it up all over his head. Immediately I wonder what I've done. What would Celeste think?

"You look awesome!" Jimmy says, jumping up and high-fiving Matthew. "Congratulations! You are now a full-on gentile boy."

Matthew grins as he takes a couple of pizza slices out of the box. "Do you like it, Selig?"

Selig studies him for a moment. "On you, maybe. But definitely not on me."

"I think you look hot," Taviana says, smiling at Matthew. "Your turn, Jon. Into the shower."

I wipe the steam off the mirror and study my head. My hair is as ridiculously and unnaturally orange as Matthew's was yellow. I try spiking it up with my fingers like Matthew did, but that's just way over the top, so I comb it out smooth. Either way, I still don't look like me, and I definitely don't look like a kid from Unity. I smile, and the strange face in the mirror smiles back. Even more than walking away from home, dyeing my hair makes me feel like I'm in control of me and not a puppet of the Prophet.

Jimmy and I shove the pizza boxes and newspaper into the recycling bins while Selig and Matthew shoot hoops. Taviana is back in the lawn chair with her book. Selig has decided against coloring his hair, and Jimmy doesn't pressure him. I've just started to wonder what Abigail will think of our hair. Will she be angry? I should have thought of that sooner. I need to stay on her good side. I have nowhere else to go.

"What are you thinking of doing that's more permanent than dyeing your hair?" I ask Jimmy as I sink into a chair beside Taviana with my own novel.

He leans against the side of the house. "Tattoo."

"Really?" Taviana looks up from her book.

"Yeah. Or a piercing. Or maybe both."

"What kind of tattoo?"

"That's the hard part. I'm trying to find a symbol that represents who I am and where I've come from. Maybe a ball and chain, with the chain broken."

I don't get what he means, but I don't say so.

"Not bad." Taviana nods. "And what would you get pierced?"

"Probably start with just an ear stud."

"Let me know when you do it," she says. "I'll come and hold your hand."

Jimmy laughs. "Thanks. I might need that."

"How much does it cost?" I ask.

They both look at me. "You want an ear stud too?" Jimmy asks.

I shrug. "Maybe."

Jimmy looks at Taviana and grins. "This from the guy who didn't want to take his shirt off tonight."

"He's coming around," she says.

Abigail and Alex return from dinner and join us in the backyard. Abigail's eyes just about bug out of her head when she sees first me and then Matthew. Alex throws back his head and laughs. "I'm surprised it took you guys so long," he says.

Abigail just stares. We smile at her as innocently as we can. "Dear God," she says finally. "Please tell me my bathroom isn't spattered in yellow and orange dye."

"No, ma'am," Jimmy says. "It's cleaner than how we found it."

"And you can thank me for that," Taviana adds. "I hate to think what might have happened if I didn't come along when I did."

Abigail sighs and ruffles my bright-orange hair before settling into a chair. Alex joins Matthew and Selig at the basketball hoop. The evening is warm, and as I watch the three of them shoot baskets, I wonder what my family is doing tonight. Evening prayers, probably. All the little ones will have been called inside for the night. Will my mother be thinking of me? Saying prayers for my lost soul? Or has she ripped my photos out of the family photo albums, determined to forget me? As an apostate, I'm supposed to be dead to her. Dead to all of them. I cringe a little, imagining her face if she could see how I look right now.

I open up my book and continue to read about Scout and Jem trying to make sense of their motherless lives.

Eight

I stare up at the wooden slats of the upper bunk. It's been seven weeks since I left Unity. My life now consists of construction work, schoolwork and gardening. Something is missing. This freedom that Jimmy promised me is way less fun than I imagined. Dyeing my hair helped—my new look makes me feel different, less like a polyg. And sure, I don't have to listen to the Prophet drone on anymore about obedience and the priesthood. But not much else has changed. I'm still a laborer, and the schoolwork is way too hard. I like my little garden here, but I had one in Unity too.

I roll over and sigh. At least in Unity I had the hope of seeing Celeste each day, even secretly. I miss that thrill, my heart fluttering in happy spasms. I also miss my family, the whole big messy mass of them, like a wild creature with many limbs yet all the parts combined to make us one. Dad was the center of that sprawling creature, but it was mom, my birth mom, who was its heart—for me, anyway.

My own heart has developed a pinprick leak, and my life feels like it is slowly dripping away, leaving me listless.

Jimmy told me that this feeling is temporary, that once I'm in school and meeting girls and taking part in stuff, I'll be glad I left home. But for now, he said, I have to get myself on track, earn some money and get caught up with school.

There was a big row in the house tonight. Matthew and Selig brought home their report cards. Matthew managed to squeak through his courses, but Selig, just as he predicted, failed everything except PE and woodwork. At first Abigail was pretty cool about it—just said that he has to go to summer school and work evening shifts at the restaurant. But Selig was totally bummed. He said summer school won't help him, that he's too stupid, and he wants to chill this summer. He's had enough school. That's when Abigail got mad. Voices were raised, and Selig stormed out of the house, slamming the door behind him. The rest of us quietly retreated to our rooms. I get how Selig feels. Abigail's rule about finishing high school might be unrealistic for us polygs.

On warm Saturdays, Craig and I meet at a picnic table in the park, shaded by trees. I'm now wearing T-shirts and shorts, though it still feels odd. Craig grinned when he first saw my orange hair. "Now you should grow it long," he said. "Wear a ponytail. Be a real rebel."

Good idea. My hair is already getting long, and my brown roots are looking kind of silly. Matthew intends to dye his again, but I'm beginning to think the ponytail idea is a better one, and I'll just let the orange grow out. Abigail has clippers that she uses to shave the boys' heads, but I'm picturing a ponytail with an orange stripe at the bottom.

"I don't get what the title has to do with the book," I tell Craig. I've finally finished reading *To Kill a Mockingbird*.

Craig picks up the book and flips through it. He reads a short passage out loud. "*Mockingbirds don't do one thing but make music for us to enjoy...but sing their hearts out for us. That's why it's a sin to kill a mockingbird.*"

"Okay, but what's that got to do with the story?"

He studies me for a moment, trying to figure out how to explain it. "Sometimes authors use symbols to make a point in the story. The mockingbird is the symbol of something innocent, something that doesn't hurt anyone. So no one should hurt them either. Who in the story could be considered innocent?"

I think about it. "Scout?"

"Yep. Anyone else? Anyone hurt by something evil?"

"Boo Radley, I guess."

"For sure. How about Tom Robinson?"

I nod, but my mind returns to the Prophet's teachings about black people. He preached that the black race brought evil. For a long time I took his word for it. I had no reason to doubt him. Now I don't know what to believe. According to this novel, it was Bob Ewell, a white guy, who was evil, and Tom Robinson, a black man, who was innocent. That's hard to get my head around, though I have no doubt that there are evil white people among us. Maybe the Prophet is one himself. He's the one who married Celeste to my father.

Craig moves on. He reads from a list of discussion questions. "*What do you think are the most important things Scout learned during this story?*"

I think about that. "She said you never really understand a person until you walk in their shoes awhile."

"That's right! Now think about your own life. Is there someone who you really don't understand?"

That's easy. "The Prophet, in Unity."

Craig laughs. "He's a complicated one."

"Do you know much about him?"

"I've been learning a few things this summer. Anyone else?"

My mind searches. I think about Celeste, and how she chose to marry my father rather than come to Springdale with me. "My friend," I say, for lack of a better term. "My friend Celeste."

Craig's brows knit together. "Celeste from Unity?"

My head jerks up. "You know her?" I'd be shocked if Celeste had talked to a gentile stranger, especially a guy, even if he was the guy building the inuksuk on the beach she was so intrigued with.

A funny look crosses his face. "I do. We've been meeting on the beach, building inuksuit together."

I look away, an intense surge of jealousy flooding through me. *I* used to meet her on the beach. *We* built inuksuit together!

He must sense a shift in my mood. "You knew her too. Obviously."

I nod. "I'm surprised she'd talk to a stranger on the beach."

"Yeah, well, she seemed uncomfortable with it at first. But I sense she's unhappy. Kind of lost. You know?"

I nod. "She's the reason I'm here," I mutter.

He leans in to hear me.

"We were meeting secretly. We were…we were in love." I've never said that out loud before. I inhale a huge breath. Papers on the table flutter as I exhale. The constant ache in my gut flares up. "We got caught. I left before I got sent away. To punish us both the Prophet immediately married her off."

"Really?"

"Yep. To my father."

"Are you kidding me?" Craig's eyes are wide. "I knew she was married, but…"

I look Craig directly in the eyes and nod.

He pushes the books aside and rests his arms and forehead on the picnic table. "Oh my god."

I swing my legs over the bench and lean against the table, staring at the river but not really seeing it.

Finally Craig lifts his head and suggests we quit for the day and go down to the beach to build inuksuit instead. I agree and shove all my books into my backpack.

We build in silence, lost in our own thoughts. When we're done, we sit on the beach to admire our work.

"Do you want me to tell her that I'm tutoring you?" he asks after a while.

I think about that. "No. There's no point."

"I've been giving her books to read," he tells me. "She sneaks them into her room and reads them at night. Then we discuss them on the beach."

It doesn't surprise me. Unlike my sisters, Celeste always questioned everything. She was a sponge for new information, and she didn't get much of it in Unity. When Taviana lived there, she filled her in on all kinds of things that happened in the outside world.

"Has she read *To Kill a Mockingbird*?"

"Not yet."

I dig out my copy, which I've had to renew twice, and hand it to him. "Get her to read it," I tell him. "And tell me what she thinks."

"Okay, I will." He shoves it into his pack.

"She was my mockingbird."

He looks at me, startled. Then he grins. "So you do get the concept of symbols." Our fingers are busy building towers with the pebbles on the beach. "Why did you mention her when I asked if there was anyone you didn't understand?"

I knock over my little tower with a flip of my hand. "She had the chance to escape the night before her marriage. She could have come to Abigail's with me. But she didn't."

"And you think you'd have to walk in her shoes to understand that?" Craig asks quietly.

I shrug. "I sort of get it. Family's everything. And she has no education. But the bottom line is, she just didn't have the guts."

"You think that's all it was?"

"Yeah, mostly. She was scared of her father. And really attached to her siblings. And her mom." My heels dig into the pebbly beach, and I bring my knees to my chest. "And maybe her father would have come here and dragged her back anyway." Actually, there are no maybes about it. Her father would have come for her. That would have been a scene.

"Did your dad try to get you to go back?"

"It's different for us guys. A lot of us have to leave anyway. If the chosen men get three or more wives, well, clearly there's not enough girls to go around. Boys have to get culled or the whole system falls apart."

Craig ignores that. "I don't know, Jon. It seems like you already get what it's like to be Celeste."

"Yeah, I guess." Or I used to know. Now I have no idea what her life is like. Married to my father. Maybe she even sits at my place at our table.

I press the heels of my palms into my eyes. Craig drapes his arm around my shoulders. "You're sure you don't want me to give her a message from you?"

I shake my head. No point stirring stuff up now.

"So," Craig says while I pull myself together, "the next book I want you to read is *The Absolutely True Diary of a Part-Time Indian* by Sherman Alexie." He takes the list of recommended reading out of my bag and points to the title. "See if you can relate to the main character in any way."

"That's a strange title for a book," I say, gathering my things.

"It is, but I think you'll find it thought provoking."

I roll my eyes. "I'm still not sure what the point is in reading novels."

Craig climbs to his feet. "It's like what Scout says. When we read novels, we get to climb into another person's skin and walk around in their bodies for a while. It increases our empathy for other people."

I'm having enough trouble walking around in my own skin these days. I don't know why I'd want to take on someone else's problems as well, but when Craig and I part, I head over to the library to see if the book's available.

I'd expected to see Taviana here, either working behind the desk at her new job or doing her schoolwork, but it's Selig's back I see at one of the computers. I walk up and tap him on the shoulder. "Hey, what's up?"

Selig quickly closes the window he's viewing. "Oh. Hi, Jon. Just surfing the Net."

"Yeah?" I notice that his skin has gone crimson. "Finding anything good?"

"No, not really." His eyes dart around, not meeting mine. "What are you doing here?"

"Craig has assigned another novel for me to read. I'm just going to check and see if it's here." I sit at the next computer and search the catalog the way Taviana taught me to. "Yep," I say. "It is. Are you busing home? Want to go together?"

"No," Selig says. "I think I'll hang out here a bit longer."

I notice he hasn't reopened the website. "You okay?" I ask.

"Yeah," he says, but the look in his eyes tells an entirely different story.

On a Friday night early in July, Abigail and Alex get up from the table after dinner and decide to go for a walk. Jimmy, Taviana, Matthew and I relax a little longer, and I listen to them making plans for the weekend. Selig is at work.

"I've got something to tell you guys, but you have to keep it a secret," Taviana says. "Promise?"

We all nod, curious.

"It's about Selig. He's not attending summer school."

"Are you sure?" Jimmy asks. "Jon and I drop him off at the school on our way to work each morning."

"I've seen him hanging around town, and he's in the library a lot," she says. "He says he's doing schoolwork, but I don't buy it. My friend Hunter, who works at the same restaurant as him, says he's done some day shifts there too."

"I saw him in the park one day," says Matthew, who's working for a landscaping company for the summer. "I asked him why he wasn't in school, and he said it was his lunch break. I thought it was odd, because it was about two o'clock in the afternoon, but I didn't figure he'd have any reason to lie."

I remember watching Abigail write him a check for his tuition. What did he do with that?

Jimmy shakes his head. "How long does he think he can get away with it? Abigail's going to find out when he's repeating all his classes in the fall."

"I doubt he's planning on going back," Taviana says.

We think about this. She's probably right. But if it's true, then he can't continue to live here.

"He's actually a really bright kid," Jimmy says. "He was just too far behind to catch up."

That's not a comforting thought.

"So who wants to talk to him?" Taviana asks.

We all look at each other, but no one volunteers.

"I think it has to be you, Jimmy," Taviana says. "You brought him here."

"I didn't *bring* him here. He was leaving anyway. I just introduced him to Abigail." He looks at her. "He likes you, Tav. Why don't you talk with him?"

"Oh no," she says. "I'm not going to play the heavy."

They both look at me. I shake my head, knowing I might be in the same trouble when I get my first report card.

"There's nothing we can say to him anyway," Jimmy says, grabbing his truck keys off the counter. "He's going to have to deal with the consequences himself."

★   ★   ★

I begin to watch Selig more closely. We continue to drop him off at the school each morning, and he makes his way home from the restaurant each night. Because he's out most evenings, he usually only sees Abigail at breakfast, and he was never much for conversation at the best of times.

"When do you find time to do your homework?" Abigail asks him one morning in the middle of July. He's staring into his cereal bowl, not making eye contact with any of us.

"I go to the library before I start work," he tells her.

"You're not finding it too much?" she asks. "Maybe you could cut back on some shifts at the restaurant."

"I'm fine," he mumbles.

"Jon's tutor might be willing to help you if you're struggling."

"I told you, I'm fine." He gets up from the table and bangs his dishes onto the counter before filling a lunch bag with food. The rest of us glance at each other, then continue to eat, but Abigail stares at his back, frowning.

"How about I drop you off at school this morning?" she says. "Then I'll check in with the teachers to see how it's going."

"Are you kidding me?" he asks, spinning around to glare at her.

"Relax, Selig. I'm just trying to help."

"Then leave me alone," he says and stomps out of the kitchen.

The rest of us finish eating and begin gathering our things for the day, but I notice that Abigail remains in her chair, staring out the window.

★   ★   ★

The summer weeks drag by. Taviana has started her courses, and because it's sweltering hot in the house, we often sit in the backyard to study at night. When it gets dark, we sit side by side under the porch light, smacking mosquitoes on our sticky arms and legs every few seconds. It's still better than working inside the house. Abigail and Alex, who have become inseparable, often go for a walk or to Alex's house so they won't disturb us. Matthew and Jimmy go swimming or out with friends, and Selig is usually at work.

One night, when it's just beginning to get dark, I hear footsteps coming down the back alley. A figure steps into the backyard. It's Selig, but there's something wrong. He appears to be staggering, and he walks right into my raised garden.

"Ouch!" he says and leans over to rub his knee.

"Are you okay?" Taviana asks.

He squints toward the house, seeing us for the first time. "Who put this friggin' garden here?" he says and then throws back his head and laughs. But the way he laughs is wrong.

Taviana walks over to him. "Have you been drinking, Selig?" she asks.

"None of your business," he says and lurches toward me.

"Selig, you're pissed!" Taviana says.

"Just had a couple beer." He slumps onto the bottom step, putting his elbows on his knees and his head into his hands. One of his elbows slides off his leg, and his whole body just about rolls forward off the step.

"They must have been pretty strong beer."

"Whatever."

"Abigail could be home any minute, Selig. I suggest you get yourself to bed before she sees you like this."

"And I suggest you quit acting like my mother." He squints at her. "I bet you've done your fair share of drinking, not to mention everything else you've done." He gives her a lewd wink.

"Selig," I say, trying to warn him. It's not like him to pick fights. The alcohol seems to have changed him.

But Taviana just seems concerned. "Selig, seriously, unless you have somewhere else to live, I suggest you get yourself to bed—and quickly."

"As a matter of fact," Selig says, "I've been working on finding a new place to live. Seattle's not so far away. I've got enough bus fare."

"What are you going to do in Seattle?" Taviana asks.

"More opportunities in a big city," he slurs.

"For a boy like you, opportunities will be limited," she tells him. "I should know. Look what happened to me when I tried to get by on my own."

"You think I'm going to be a hooker?" he asks. His eyes go wide and he honks out a laugh, but there's no humor in it.

"Selig," I say one more time, but I realize how useless I sound.

"There's a market for boys like you," she tells him.

"Well, I don't give a flying fuck," he says, which is totally out of character for him. "I'm damned for all eternity anyway. Just like you are, Jon." He gets to his feet and tries to maneuver up the stairs. "I'm a worthless, stupid piece of shit, and I don't really care what happens anymore."

"That's ridiculous, Selig," Taviana says. "Don't say things like that. You're going through a rough patch, that's all. Things will work out. They will." She puts her arm around him, but he shrugs it off.

"Easy for you to say." He pushes the door open with his shoulder and practically falls into the house.

Taviana and I follow him inside and watch as he lurches down the hall to his bedroom.

"I hope he doesn't get sick in the night," Taviana says.

It's a rough-looking Selig that climbs into the truck the next morning. He slept in and missed breakfast, but fortunately Abigail seemed preoccupied. When we get to the school he climbs out of the truck and looks back at me. It's the first eye contact he's made this morning, and he has the look of a stray dog who's been kicked and beaten until he's lost his trust in humans.

"Have a good day, Selig," Jimmy says.

Selig just stands there, hands shoved in pockets, waiting for us to leave so he can walk away from the school. I wonder if he'll find somewhere to sleep it off. As soon as we pull away, I tell Jimmy about the previous night. He just sighs and shakes his head. We drive to the job site in silence.

★ ★ ★

Craig and I are working at the picnic bench. He's quizzing me on the elements in the periodic table when I see a familiar girl walking through the park. She glances over at us and then does a double take.

"Jon-without-an-*h*!" she says, tottering over to the table. She's wearing sandals with a wedge heel, a bikini top and cutoff shorts. The button above the fly has been left undone.

"Hi, Belle." I see Craig glance at me curiously.

"I hardly recognized you. You've...changed your hair," she says.

I nod, trying to maintain eye contact, but it's hard with the way she's busting out of the bikini top, which is right at eye level with my position on the bench.

"Where have you been hiding?" she asks. "I keep asking Jimmy. He just says you've been busy."

"Yeah, well, that's the truth. Working and studying."

"Sounds like a boring existence. Why don't you come out at night with him anymore?"

I shrug.

Her attention turns to Craig. She sticks out her hand. "Hi, I'm Belle."

Craig shakes her hand and smiles. "Craig."

She's beaming. "You should come out too."

I don't know how to respond or where to look. Finally I turn to Craig. "I guess we'd better get back to work."

She gets the hint. "Jimmy knows how to get hold of me when you decide to have some fun," she says, smiling. "Nice meeting you, Craig." She turns and bounces across the park.

"I wouldn't have thought she was your type," Craig says, smiling.

I feel my face burn. "I only met her once, the second night I was here."

"She's really friendly."

"Yeah."

"I think she likes you."

Funny. Jimmy said the exact same thing.

Nine

"So I totally get why you thought I should read this novel," I tell Craig. "Arnold's like me, stuck between two ways of life."

July has rolled into August, and there's only a few weeks before school starts. We're at our usual picnic table, discussing *The Absolutely True Diary of a Part-Time Indian*. I read so slowly that I've only completed two of the suggested novels.

"I thought you might identify with him."

"Yeah, but there's one big difference. Arnold gets to go back and forth. I'm here for good, whether it works out or not."

Craig nods, waiting. I've grown used to his way of tutoring. He doesn't instruct so much as listen carefully and then ask thoughtful questions.

"And my life in Unity wasn't as hard as his was in Wellpinit."

"*Would you say Arnold was suffering a life-changing identity crisis?*" He's reading from a list of discussion questions again.

"I don't know what that means."

"Well, what do you think his main problem was?"

I think about that. Poor Arnold had a lot of problems. He had health issues, his family was a mess, and he was bullied. But mostly he was trying to figure out where he fit in, at the reservation or in Reardan, where the white kids went to school. "I guess he was trying to figure out where he belonged."

"Exactly." He studies my face. "Does Unity have anything in common with Wellpinit?"

"Are you kidding? Alcohol is forbidden in Unity."

"That's just one aspect. Think some more."

I stare out at the river, struggling to find anything the two towns have in common. "Well, they're both isolated from the rest of the world."

"Good point. Anything else?"

"There's strong family connections, I guess."

"So what does Arnold ultimately decide? Where does he fit in?"

"He decides he's not just Indian or just white. He belongs to many tribes."

Craig studies me for a moment. "Can you apply that to your life?"

I just shrug.

"Well, you grew up in Unity," he says, trying to encourage me, "and now you're here."

"Actually, I think it's different for me. I was a polyg, and now I'm not. Unlike Arnold, I don't belong in both places."

"I think you're wrong about that, Jon. You grew up in Unity, where there are strong family values as well as strong religious ones. That will always be a part of you. You'll always be able to empathize with other people you meet who have come from different backgrounds."

"Did Celeste read *To Kill a Mockingbird*?" I ask.

"She did. We had some great discussions about it."

"Did she understand what the title meant?"

He nods. "After we talked about it for a bit."

"What else did she think about it?"

Craig is quiet for a moment, clearly trying to remember. "For some reason it prompted a conversation about religion. She asked what makes people behave if they don't believe in God."

"What did you tell her?"

"I assured her that there are many good, kind and well-behaved people who don't believe in God."

"Did she believe you?"

"I don't know. She says that when you submit to a higher power, life is easier, because all your decisions are made for you. That leads to happiness."

"What did you say?"

"I told her that there are some things more important than just being happy."

"Like what?"

"Like being free to think for yourself."

"Did she agree?"

"I'm not sure, but the books are definitely opening her mind to new ways of thinking."

I start packing the textbooks into my backpack.

"School starts in a couple of weeks, Jon. How are you feeling about that?"

"Not very good," I tell him.

"How come?"

"I saw what happened to Selig. He flunked out. And I'm sure I'm going to get bullied because of where I came from. That's something else I'll have in common with Arnold."

"Did Matt and Selig get picked on?"

"They haven't talked much about it."

"Arnold was a fighter. You can fight back too, just not with your fists."

"Will you keep on tutoring me?"

He shakes his head. "I'm going to university in a couple of weeks."

"Really? You never said anything about that."

"I know. It's odd, but it was your friend Celeste that got me thinking about it. We ended up talking about religion and spirituality so much that I decided I wanted to study theology."

"Theology?"

"The study of religion."

"*You* want to study religion?"

He laughs. "I'm not studying to become someone like your Prophet. I just want a better understanding of all the world religions."

"You don't seem like a religious person to me."

"That depends on your definition of religion. I don't call any one religion my own, but I feel like a spiritual person. And Buddhism interests me."

I have no idea what Buddhism is.

"But honestly, Jon, I think I have done what I set out to do with you."

"And what's that?" I haven't come close to finishing all the chapters in the science and math textbooks like he said I would.

"I've turned you into a reader."

"You think so?"

"Yeah, these novels have helped you learn as much about life as the stuff you'll learn in those science textbooks."

I look at him, unconvinced.

"Don't get me wrong. Science and math are important too. And so is history. But good novels will open your mind, change your thinking."

"It won't be the same without you to discuss them with."

"I'll be back next summer. We can start up again then. But in the meantime, we have a couple more weeks. I'll let you choose the next novel."

I get up and swing my pack over my shoulder, but Craig remains seated at the picnic bench, looking serious.

"You okay?"

"There's something I think I should tell you, Jon. About Celeste."

"What is it?"

"I wasn't going to mention it, but then I thought you might hear it from someone else, maybe another guy who leaves Unity."

I note that he doesn't use the term Lost Boy.

"And I thought you'd rather hear it from me."

"Is she okay?"

"Yes. She's okay. Not particularly happy, I'd say, but she's being treated well."

"Then what is it?"

He looks directly at me. "She's having a baby."

I collapse back down to the bench and drop my head onto the table. Craig comes around and puts his hand on my shoulder, but he doesn't say anything else.

★ ★ ★

When Craig leaves, I find my shady spot under the weeping willow by the river. The kicked-in-the gut feeling has shifted, and now I want to pick up one of the boulders on the beach and hurl it at God. How could He let this happen?

I slump to the ground and cover my head with my arms, trying to push away the images of my father with Celeste, but they only grow stronger—images of him lying with her, doing all the things I wanted to do. He didn't even love her the way I did. For him it was just another girl to have sex with, to produce more children so he could achieve the highest realm in heaven. It's all about his place in heaven. Suddenly I hate him. I want to claw and hit and kill him.

I lie back and let out a long wail, then let tears spill unchecked.

After a while the tears dry up, and I notice the anger has

melted away. A dull ache settles over me. Deep down, I knew this would happen, but I refused to think about it.

Celeste's baby will be another brother or sister for me. How many is that now? Wasn't Mother Sarah expecting one when I left home? It doesn't matter. I'm not likely to see any of them ever again.

★ ★ ★

As soon as I open the door, I sense tension in the house. Matthew and Taviana are standing in the kitchen, looking pale. "What?" I ask.

Before either of them can answer, I hear a bedroom door slam, and Selig comes down the hall, carrying his backpack. It's bursting at the seams. He throws it over his shoulder.

"What's going on?" I ask him.

"I'm leaving," he says.

"Where are you going?"

"Brent and Charlie have a couch I can sleep on, just until I earn a little more money." Brent and Charlie are also former polygs, who rent an apartment together near the town center. They're older than us, and they've been out longer. I've heard they've resorted to selling drugs to help pay the rent. I've also heard they party pretty hard.

The porch door opens and Abigail comes into the kitchen from the backyard. Her face is blotchy from crying. Selig turns to leave.

"Selig," she says.

He stops but doesn't turn around. The kitchen grows completely still, but no one says anything. Eventually Abigail breaks the silence. "Keep in touch, Selig." Her voice is hoarse. "I'll be praying for you."

He turns at that, regards her for a moment and walks back across the room. He hesitates and then pulls her into a clumsy hug. She wraps both arms around his skinny frame. They hold each other like this for few moments before he breaks away, swats at his eyes and, without another word, turns and goes out the front door.

Abigail drops into a chair, slouches forward, and the room becomes quiet again. "He wasn't attending school," she says.

I glance at Taviana and Matthew, wondering who ratted him out.

"Charlie is his cousin," she continues. "At least he'll have a roof over his head." She releases a huge sigh. "I always feel like I've failed when this happens. But I can't make exceptions."

Jimmy's truck pulls into the driveway, and a moment later he comes into the house. "What happened?" he asks, taking in the sad faces.

"Selig's gone," Abigail says.

"Gone?"

"Moved out."

"Oh." Jimmy sits in a chair beside Abigail and puts his arm around her. "You did your best," he assures her.

She covers her face with her hands. "Did I? Maybe it was too much to ask him to complete school. Maybe he really couldn't do it."

"Maybe he just doesn't realize how important it is," Jimmy says. "When he's been on his own for a while, he may decide to try again."

"It will only get harder the more time that passes," she says.

"Well, maybe by then he'll be able to complete the work online, like Tavi is doing, and go at his own pace."

The room goes quiet again. No one really believes that will happen.

"I'll make supper," Taviana says and opens the fridge.

"I'll get some vegetables from the garden," I offer.

Jimmy follows me outside. "What happened?" he asks as I pull up carrots.

"I don't know. I got home right before you. Selig was heading out the door."

"There must have been quite the fight between Selig and Abigail."

"I know. The way Taviana and Matthew looked when I came in the door, you'd think someone had died or something."

"Abigail was the best chance Selig had," Jimmy says, breaking a red pepper from its stem. "Nothing good will happen at Charlie and Brent's."

Ten

I flip through the pages of the biology textbook before I pack it into the bag with the others. I only completed nine of the fifteen chapters. Math was worse—I got through less than half of that textbook, and even fewer chapters in the physics one. Even with that, I don't remember much of what I read. School starts tomorrow, and I'm totally not ready. Did Mrs. Kennedy really expect that I could get through all that shit in just one summer? I wasted my time reading novels—I should have been reading the textbooks instead. Stories aren't going to help me pass an algebra exam or help me understand ecology and ecosystems. Why did Craig insist I read them? The Prophet may be right about novels. I flop on my bed and pull my pillow over my face.

Craig said Celeste gobbled up the books he brought her. We even went to a used bookstore before he left, and I watched him choose more for her to read over the fall and winter. I can't imagine how she gets them into her house—my house—where kids and mothers are everywhere. She must tuck them into the folds of her dress and sneak them in, one at a time, and then stash them in a good hiding place.

Well, Celeste doesn't have to learn geometry or memorize senseless grammar rules. I guess I could have cut back on the hours I worked this summer in order to study more, but the money was too good, and it felt sweet to do something physical and that comes easily. Abigail helped me open a bank account and explained what interest is. I love seeing how quickly my balance grows, even after paying her for my keep.

Craig left for university last week. He showed me how to set up an email account on the library computer so we can stay in touch. He suggested I use my savings to buy a cell phone so we could text each other, but I can't see why I would. Emailing is free.

"You're looking pretty glum tonight, Jon." Taviana passes me the garlic bread.

I just shrug. We're all at the table, eating supper. Alex has taken over Selig's place.

"Worried about school?" Abigail asks.

"Yeah, I guess. A bit."

"The good thing about school," Jimmy says, "is that there's way more girls there than on the job site. No offense, sir," he says to Alex.

"No offense taken," Alex says between mouthfuls.

I nod and try to smile. I know Jimmy's just trying to cheer me up. But it's easy for him. He doesn't start school tomorrow.

"What about you, Matthew?" Abigail says. "This will be your last year," she reminds him. "Unless you go on to college."

Matthew just nods and reaches for another piece of bread.

Abigail wipes her mouth and pushes her chair back. "Well, Alex and I want to support you boys as best as we can. With that in mind, Alex brought you something that I think will cheer you up. You too, Taviana." She nods at Alex, who smiles back at her. "Go on—take a look in Selig's old room."

I look at Matthew and then Taviana. They are as puzzled as I am. Together we head down to the end of the hall. In Selig's vacated bedroom, a desk has been set up under the window with a laptop computer and a printer on it. We look back at Abigail and Alex, who are watching us from the hallway, big smiles plastered on their faces.

"I've recently upgraded my work laptop," Alex says. "I needed something with more memory, but this one still works fine. I thought the three of you might be able to use it for your studies. Abigail bought the printer to go with it. Cable for Internet access will be installed this week."

"Hopefully you can use it during the day, Taviana," Abigail says, "so it's free for the boys in the evening."

"*You* might even want to use it in the evenings," Alex teases. He throws his arm around her shoulders and pulls her in.

She rolls her eyes. "What for? My sewing machine is all I need."

We take turns thanking Alex and hugging Abigail.

"Can I fire it up?" Matthew asks.

"It's all yours," Alex says. "I'm going back to the kitchen to see if there's any leftover lasagna."

"Me too," Jimmy says, following Alex down the hall.

Matthew sits in the desk chair and opens the laptop. He presses the power switch, and Taviana and I watch as the computer comes to life. I appreciate that Abigail and Alex are trying to help us, but I really don't know how a computer is going to help me memorize capital cities or figure out what exponential functions are.

Lists with every student's name and homeroom are posted inside the front entrance of the school. I find mine, and Matthew helps me locate the classroom.

"It's going to be okay," he says. "Your homeroom teacher will hand you a sheet with the rest of your courses and their room numbers. Just sit at the back of each classroom and stay under the radar. I'll meet you in the cafeteria at noon." He gives me a light punch on the shoulder and then joins the buzzing swarm of students moving through the hallways.

My first stop is at Mrs. Kennedy's office to return the textbooks. She seems genuinely happy to see me. "Wow, Jon," she says, looking me over. "You look...different."

I just smile as I think about who I was when I met her last spring. Still wearing my polyg clothes, with my tidy haircut and pale skin.

"Come by to see me anytime," she calls as I head down the corridor.

Biology is my first class after homeroom, and I find the classroom easily enough. I take Matthew's advice and sit in a desk at the back. From there I watch the other kids enter the room. The weather is still warm, so everyone is dressed much as they were last spring. I'm wearing shorts and a T-shirt, and my hair has grown long enough to pull into a ponytail like Craig's. I don't think anyone would know by looking at me that I was a polyg. That brings me some comfort, but I can't hide the fact that I'm older than most of these kids, almost eighteen. I'm probably the tallest person in the room, and I've got a strong build from working in construction all summer. I even have to shave every few days. They'll wonder what I'm doing here. I sink lower in my chair.

A guy plants himself into the desk next to mine, dropping his backpack to the floor between us. Our eyes meet for a moment before I go back to doodling on a fresh sheet of paper.

"New here?" I hear him ask.

I nod but don't look at him. I'm staying under the radar.

"Where are you from?"

My mind freezes. I wish I'd thought this through. Should

I tell him the truth or make something up? "Highrock," I say, deciding on the latter.

"I attended Highrock Secondary at the start of last year," he says. "I don't remember you."

I shrug, but my ears are burning.

"You sure you're not from Unity?" he asks. "There's something about you…"

My ears get even hotter. I glance around to see if anyone has heard him. Should I dig myself in deeper and deny it or just ignore him? Again I choose the latter and continue to doodle.

"Hey, it's not like I care," the guy says. "I'm dealing with my own shit. Just wondering, that's all."

I finally look over. At first glance he's tough-looking, with sleeve tattoos up both arms, a shaved head and a row of gold rings protruding out of his left eyebrow. But when I meet his eyes, I see something else—a wounded kid under that hard shell. I'm way too familiar with wounded boys—Unity is full of them.

I still don't answer him, but in that moment of eye contact, I feel we've made some kind of connection.

"Wolf," he says.

"Wolf?"

"That's my name. Short for Wolfgang. Like I said, I've got my own shit to deal with."

"I'm Jon," I say, and then add, "Without an *h*."

The teacher closes the door with a bang, and my first biology class begins.

* ★ ★

"So, how was the morning?" Matthew asks. We're seated at a table in the cafeteria, unwrapping sandwiches. Cafeteria food isn't in our budget.

I don't have the words to describe the hopelessness that's been building in me all morning, so I don't say anything.

Matthew looks up from his sandwich, but before he can ask anything else, a group of his twelfth-grade friends descend on our table, trays banging down and the boys jostling to make room on the benches. I scoot down to one end, and Matthew is at the other. He looks at me apologetically. I just shrug, feeling completely invisible. Not one of his friends has acknowledged my presence. I look around the cafeteria and see Wolf in a back corner. He has a book propped open on the table in front of him and appears to be reading while he eats.

When I finish my lunch, I get up and walk around and around the school grounds, wishing I was anywhere but here.

★ ★ ★

"So?" Taviana asks when I get home. "How was your first day?"

"Fucked." I throw my backpack on the couch and reach for the TV remote. I can feel her standing in the kitchen doorway, staring at me.

I flick through the stations, not really seeing anything. I'm aware of her still standing there and begin to feel a little bad about my reaction.

"I met a guy named Wolf," I tell her. "He says he's from Highrock. You know him?"

She nods. "He's younger than me, but I know who he is."

"He knew just by looking at me that I was a polyg."

"So?" She shrugs. "You're not one anymore."

It's not just the clothes we wear. Our people have a certain look, a similarity—which only makes sense, seeing as we're all pretty much related. "He says he doesn't care, because he has his own shit to deal with."

"It's not just in Unity that families have issues. He's probably impressed that you've escaped your past. Maybe he'd like to run away from his family too."

I think about that. Maybe. I turn off the TV and go outside to pull weeds from my vegetable garden. The combination of fresh air, the warm soil and the feel of a plump, ripe tomato resting in the palm of my hand soothes my jangled nerves.

The back door bangs shut, and Jimmy leaps from the top stair down to the yard in one bound. "Meet any girls?" he asks, scooping up a basketball and taking a long shot. The ball hits the rim and bounces away.

I place the vegetables I've gathered on the picnic table and snag the ball out of the air after his next shot. "Not yet, but I met a Wolf."

He gives me a surprised look. "Well, that sounds promising!"

★ ★ ★

"Anyone sitting here?"

Wolf is eating alone at the corner table again. "Doesn't look like it," he says and turns the page of his book.

I sit down and unwrap my lunch.

He shows me the cover of his book. *A Feast for Crows.* "Have you read it?"

I shake my head.

"Have you read the first books in the series?"

"I don't read much."

He looks surprised, but then he gets it. He remembers where I'm from. "You should—they based a season of *Game of Thrones* on this book. It's the fourth in a series. All the books are awesome."

I nod, but there's not a chance. I'm never going to be able to keep up with the reading for my classes as it is.

A girl suddenly plunks herself down next to Wolf. "Hi," she says and smiles at both of us. The braces on her teeth glint.

We just gaze back at her. Her long brown hair is pulled into a loose knot on the top of her head. She's wearing ripped shorts, a turquoise blouse and sneakers. Hoop earrings dangle from her earlobes. She has a pretty face, but I've yet to get used to the fashion of these girls.

She turns. "Is your name really Wolf?"

Wolf nods.

There's an eruption of giggles at the next table. A bunch of girls are watching us, hands over their mouths as they try to conceal their laughter.

"They dared me to come and sit with you guys," the girl admits.

"Well, aren't you the brave one, sitting with a Wolf," Wolf says loudly so the girls at the next table can hear.

That sets them off again. I take a closer look. Probably ninth grade. Lots of makeup, short shorts and wispy blouses.

"You guys want to hang out?" the girl asks.

Wolf looks at me. I just shrug.

"We're going to shoot some hoops," Wolf says, giving me a nod that says *just go along with it*. "Do you think your friends would like to have a little pickup game?"

She looks over at them. They glance at each other, hoping someone else will make a decision.

"Okay, it's decided then," Wolf says. "Let's go find us a ball."

Wolf and I lead the pack of giggling girls down the hall to the gym, where we sign out a basketball. A couple more girls have joined our group by the time we reach the outside court. Wolf divides us into two teams, him on one, me on the other. The girls are divided according to hair color. The fairest three are on my team, and the darker-haired ones on his. He throws me the ball, and I dribble it toward a hoop. I look for a girl to pass it to, but they are all hanging back, so I shoot the ball and it drops into the basket. The fair girls cheer. Wolf grabs the ball and dribbles it the other way. He teases

the girls, dribbling circles around them and not-so-acciden-
tally bumping into them, which sets off peals of laughter. I can't
help but smile at his strategy. He shoots and also scores.

Slowly the girls get into the game. I can't bring myself to
purposely bump into any of them the way Wolf does, but one
pushes up against me as I wait to receive a pass. Once I have the
ball, I hold it over my head, looking for someone to throw it to.
The girl leaps against me, over and over, trying to knock the ball
out of my hands. I'm way taller than her, and she doesn't come
anywhere close to the ball, but her body repeatedly brushes
against mine. It seems no one has taught these girls that body
checking is not allowed in basketball. Wolf grins at me.

When the bell rings, Wolf snatches the ball from one of the
girls and dribbles it back toward the gym. Crystal, the girl who
first joined our table at lunch, walks with me into the school.

"Are you in eleventh grade with Wolf?" she asks.

"Yeah."

"You look older."

I don't answer, but my heart sinks. For a short time I felt
like I was fitting in.

"Well, see you around," she says and jogs off to class.

I wait for Wolf, and he gives me a high five. "So now you've
met some girls," he says. "School life is about to improve."

Lunch hours with Wolf and the girls are a nice distrac-
tion from failed quizzes, well-meaning teachers who want

to help but can't and a growing pile of work that I do not understand. By the end of the third week of September, my worry about catching up has mushroomed into full-on despair. I try to be invisible. I sit in the back of each class, but I know that even though I dress like the rest of them, I still stand out, being a full two years older and a head taller. The teachers ramble on about scientific studies and theories, numerical analysis and the significance of historical events. I often feel like I've been dropped into a classroom in a foreign country where I don't know the language or even how I got there. As I predicted, the home computer hasn't been any help either.

I'm back in biology class on a Friday afternoon late in September. The teacher has asked us to find a partner and quiz each other on the parts of the respiratory system. Wolf pulls his desk up next to mine.

"I'll quiz you first," he says. He reads from the textbook. *"What is the nasal cavity, and what does it do?"*

"The nose. And it takes in air."

"Good. The epiglottis?"

I shake my head. I read the chapter last night, but none of the words registered in my brain.

"It's the flap that prevents food from falling into your trachea," Wolf says.

I have no idea what a trachea is.

"How about the glottis? Same word as epiglottis without the epi part."

I stare at the floor.

"Opening between the vocal cords," he says. I feel his eyes on me for a moment and then he hands me the textbook. "You quiz me."

I find the list of respiratory parts and sound them out as best as I can.

"The pah-har-x."

"The pharynx," he corrects. "Food and air pass through the pharynx before reaching their destinations. The pharynx also plays a role in speech."

"Why do we even need to know this shit?"

"Just because," he says. "Continue."

"The lar-y-nix."

"Larynx. It's essential for speech."

"Bron-chi."

"Bron-*kai*. The bronchi branch from the trachea into each lung and create the network of passages that supply the lungs with air."

"You know this stuff already." I hand the book back to him.

He shrugs. "I'm good at memorizing."

The only stuff I've ever had to memorize was Scripture, and I wasn't any good at that either. Maybe if it had made some sense...

"Do you want me to help you with this?" he asks.

A flush of anger burns in my gut. How is it he can memorize these facts when I can't? They just get jumbled together in my brain, along with all the material from my other classes. Respiratory-system terms get mixed up with chemistry terms. Math concepts tangle with physics ones. No wonder Selig dropped out.

"There's no point," I tell him. "I can't do it."

"You're going to have to. It's the only way to pass."

I reach over, take the textbook from him and snap it shut.

He just shrugs again. "Let me know if you change your mind." The legs of his desk scrape the floor as he returns it to its proper place in the row.

All around the room everyone is working in pairs, heads bowed to study the diagram in the book. Back in Unity, these kids would be out working, the boys mostly in construction and the girls helping their mothers with household chores, and waiting to hear who the Prophet would assign them to in marriage.

What am I doing here? I grab my backpack and stomp across the classroom and out the door. No one tries to stop me. I walk straight to the school office and down the hall to Mrs. Kennedy's room. She's sitting at her desk and looks up, startled, when I step in.

"Oh, Jon! What is it?"

"I can't do it." I start pulling the textbooks out of my backpack and pile them on her desk.

"But Jon, it's only been three weeks. You haven't given school a chance."

"Oh yes I have. I've learned that I'm stupid. Algebra makes no sense at all. I can't read or write well enough to get through English. I'm done." I place the final textbook on her desk with a bang before turning to leave.

"Jon. Stop!"

Following orders. That's something I know how to do. It's ingrained in me. I stop walking, but I don't turn around.

Mrs. Kennedy gets up and closes her office door. "Have a seat," she says, and instead of returning to the other side of her desk she pulls a second chair up to face the one I first sat in three months ago. We both sit down. "Tell me what's happening."

"Nothing's happening except there's too much to learn."

"Are you making friends?"

"Sort of. One." I don't think the girls qualify as friends. They're more like amusements, and their behavior makes me a little uncomfortable. With the exception of Taviana, I'm not used to such assertive girls.

The room goes quiet for a moment. I feel the need to fill the silence. "I can't do it. I appreciate your trying to help, but it's no good. I'm quitting."

"Jon," she says quietly. "This has nothing to do with being stupid or smart. You have simply not been given the building blocks that new information depends on. If you had been taught more than Scripture in the early grades, you'd have a solid base now, the foundation to learn more."

I know about solid bases. From building houses. "Well, I don't have the right foundation, so there's no point talking about it."

We sit quietly for another moment.

"Did you feel stupid when you studied with Craig this summer?" Mrs. Kennedy asks.

I shake my head. Craig had a way of making new information interesting, even exciting. He told me about things I never knew existed, like dinosaurs and prehistoric humans. He showed me pictures of amazing things—an astronaut walking on the moon—and he opened my mind to possibilities in medicine. What he didn't do was catch me up on high school math and science.

"What you need, Jon, is an individualized learning program." She sighs. "Unfortunately, we don't have the funding to support that."

"I don't need any more schooling to build houses."

"I want you to reach your potential. And you need an education to do that."

Her kindness is making things even harder. I stare out the window at a tree in the distance and will the tears away. It doesn't work. I swipe at my eyes, grab my almost-empty pack and head out the door.

PART
TWO

Eleven

Charlie tosses me a beer, and I snag it out of the air. I shouldn't have another one. I've already had a few and have to work in the morning, but I'm the only one here who has to get up early, so it's not like I'm going to get any sleep anyway. The couch is my bed, and it's groaning under the weight of the people crowded on it. Now I know why this place is called a butt hut.

I crack the tab and take a long swig. It didn't take me long to figure out that beer numbs everything. Shots of tequila work even better, but after spending a morning puking my guts out behind a job site, I've learned to refrain from the hard stuff on work nights.

Selig and Brent are sitting on the floor in front of the TV, playing video games. I'm on the couch watching, my arm around Belle. She's snuggled in deep. Pot always makes her mellow. I hope she's planning to stay all night on this couch with me.

The boys have strung Christmas lights around the apartment, and a little plastic tree hunches forlornly in one corner, but no one ever remembers to plug in the lights. I have no clue what Belle means when she calls it a Charlie Brown tree, and I've quit asking people to explain these references. It just reminds them that I'm still a Unity newbie.

I look around the room at the faces of the other Lost Boys and their stoned girlfriends. I'd felt like such a failure when I first crashed here. Just another loser polyg. It was going to be a short stay. I was going to prove everyone wrong—that I could make it on my own, without a high school diploma— but these guys have become family, the same way Matthew, Jimmy and Taviana were family at Abigail's. Family is everything, especially when you no longer have anything else to believe in. Unlike Arnold—the "part-time Indian" from the novel who learned he belonged in both his worlds—we don't belong in either Unity or Springdale. But we have each other. Besides, construction work slows down when the winter weather hits. Work is sporadic, and my savings are nearly gone. I can't afford to live anywhere else.

"You look like hell," Jimmy says. He still picks me up on the days when Alex has work for both of us.

"Thanks."

He shakes his head. "You don't smell very good either."

I ignore him. "Could you pull into the drive-through? I haven't had any breakfast." I didn't have any dinner last night either, but I don't bother mentioning that.

I look down at Jimmy's lunch bag sitting on the bench seat between us.

"Yeah," he says, before I can ask. "I packed you a sandwich."

"Thanks."

"And Taviana says to say hi. She still wants to connect with you."

"I know. Tell her I'll be in touch." I've been saying that for two months. "Anything new?" I ask.

"Yeah. I got accepted into Highrock Community College. I start in January."

"Cool," I say, trying to sound happy for him, but a stab of jealousy makes my gut clench. Jimmy is one of the few polygs who managed to get through school. "Still want to be a social worker?"

"Maybe. I'll see where it takes me."

I think back to the conversation we had six months ago. It feels more like ten years ago. I was a different person then. So hopeful. So friggin' naïve.

Jimmy pulls into the fast-food chain's drive-through. "The usual?" he asks.

I nod and wait while Jimmy orders. We drive to the takeout window, and the girl leans over so she can see me in the passenger seat. Her boobs spill out of her uniform. "Hi, Jon," she says.

"Hey, Olivia."

Jimmy gives me a look and then hands her a ten-dollar bill. She passes him the bag of food and change. I wave as we pull away and then open the bag. "Thanks," I mumble.

"You're welcome. Who was that?"

"Just a girl."

Jimmy waits for more, but I don't offer any. The truth is, she's one of Charlie's customers and hangs out at the apartment sometimes.

"I won't be able to spring for your food any longer," Jimmy says. "I'll be in school the rest of the winter. I won't be able to work again until after the spring term. I need to save everything I've got."

"You won't be working anymore?"

"Can't," he says. "I'll be at school every day."

My mind is fuzzy this morning, but not so fuzzy that I don't hear a little alarm bell go off. Without Jimmy to drive me, it'll be a lot more trouble, almost impossible, to get to some job sites.

"Hello, boys," Alex says when we arrive at the home where we'll be working on a bathroom renovation. It's a fortress of a house, high on the hill overlooking Springdale.

"Hey," I say, but I don't meet his eyes.

"Did you get a good sleep last night, Jon?" he asks.

"Sure did," I answer. He was on my case about my work

on our last job, calling it shoddy. I'd apologized with the excuse that I was tired.

Which I was.

We get our instructions from Alex. I try to stay focused as I measure and cut, but it's hard. Belle did stay over last night, and we had a mind-blowing couple of hours alone on the couch. The hangover is the price paid—and well worth it.

I remember the day Alex told me I still had a job with him. There'd been a big scene at Abigail's when I told them I'd quit school. They each pleaded with me to give it another chance, but I knew it was hopeless. Abigail didn't have to ask me to go. She simply went into the backyard while I packed up my few things. Jimmy, Matthew and Taviana stood at the door and watched me leave after Alex told me that he'd still see me at work. His eyes were glassy too. I'm glad they couldn't see the tears streaming down my face as I walked away.

It wasn't hard to find Selig. He was still working at the restaurant, and Brent and Charlie were willing to take me in too, even though their apartment is a steady stream of people crashing for a few nights or a few weeks. It's a rare night that there's no one else sleeping in the living room, so I had to make the most of having it to myself last night. Just me and Belle.

I poke around the enormous kitchen while Jimmy finishes his sandwiches at the table. Music blasts through his iPod. Alex has gone off to supervise on another job site, and the owners of this home are at work. It's nice when it's just the two of us on a project. We don't have to compromise about what music to listen to or when to take our breaks.

"These people are friggin' rich," I say.

"Yeah."

I open up the enormous fridge and scan the contents. "There's more food in here than in my old house in Unity, and there we had twenty-five-plus people under one roof."

Jimmy doesn't answer, but I know he's watching me.

"Do you think they'd mind if I helped myself to a glass of milk?" I ask.

"Stick to water, Jon," he says. "From the sink."

I ignore him. "They'll never notice that one glass of milk is missing," I say as I reach for the jug. "They've got two of these."

"*Thou shalt not steal*," Jimmy says. "How fast you've forgotten your boyhood lessons." He begins to pack up the lunch containers.

I pretend not to hear him as I chug back a glass of milk. I'd forgotten how good it tastes. I refill the glass and start opening cupboard doors, amazed at the kinds of food they store. No home canning here. There are expensive-looking pasta sauces, an array of oils and vinegars, and all kinds of fancy-looking chocolate. They don't just have peanut butter— they have almond and cashew butter too, and more shapes of pasta than I've ever seen. There are cookies, protein powder and a variety of crispy snacking food.

"Quit snooping," Jimmy says. There's an edge to his voice now.

"It's not hurting anyone." I open another closet. "Holy shit!" The shelves are lined with wine racks full of bottles, and not just wine bottles. "Looks like a friggin' liquor store."

"How would you know? You're underage. You've never even been in one."

"It's how I imagine one would look." I pull out a bottle of Irish whiskey and study the label. "Aged eight years, whatever that means. The butt hut would be impressed."

Jimmy doesn't say anything, but he's still staring at me.

"The rich get richer, and the poor get poorer," I say.

Something crosses Jimmy's face.

"What?" I say.

He just shakes his head. "We'd better get back to work."

"No. Tell me what you were thinking." I'm still gripping the bottle of whiskey, wondering how I can sneak it out of here.

"I'm thinking that maybe I won't be such a good social worker after all. The failures are too hard to accept."

I stare at him, his message slowly sinking in. "You're calling me a failure?"

"All I know is you're not the same guy who left Abigail's two and a half months ago. That guy knew his place."

"And what place is that?"

"You know exactly what I mean. You'd better put the booze and milk back before someone shows up."

"Don't go acting all superior, Jimmy," I tell him, seething. "You're an apostate like the rest of us, damned for all eternity. Following God's commandments isn't going to help any of us now. We're all going to burn in hell anyway."

Jimmy's eyes grow wide. "Who the hell have you been listening to?"

"People who get me a lot better than you ever did. Selig and I didn't stand a chance here, and you damn well knew it. You should have left us alone."

Jimmy gets up from the table and steps over to me. He reaches for the bottle, but I hold it behind me. "Don't you dare put the blame on me," he says, his voice raised. I've never seen him lose his cool before. "You had as good a chance as anyone, but you're a quitter. You had us to support you. The school would have supported you. Craig supported you. There were all kinds of people who would have helped you get through, but you blew us all off."

"I couldn't do it."

"Do you think it was easy for me?" He's practically screaming now, his voice matched by the angry music blaring in the background. "It was friggin' hard! And Matthew is barely hanging on, but he's a fighter. He knows what he wants, and he's going to get it." Jimmy tries again to grab the bottle from my hand, but I step back. "You let self-pity derail you, Jon. All that moping about for Celeste. What were you thinking? She's from Unity! She was never going to leave. You were an idiot to get tangled up with her in the first place. Now she's just another ignorant sister wife."

He shakes his head and starts strapping on his tool belt. Something in me snaps.

"Don't you dare talk about Celeste like that!" I swing the bottle at him, but he ducks back, and it connects with the corner of a cupboard and breaks. The bottle smashes into shards of glass as it hits the tile floor. The room fills with the pungent fumes of whiskey.

"Now you've done it," Jimmy says.

"Done what?" Alex asks, stepping into the kitchen. Neither of us heard him come into the house. I watch his face as he takes in the mess, the glass rubble, the puddle of booze on the counter, dripping to the floor, the milk jug, the broken neck of the bottle still in my hand. "What the…?" he says.

He stares at me and then at Jimmy. I can feel how hard I'm breathing, but the anger is draining away, and now shame courses through me. Jimmy steps over to the table and shuts off the music.

"I'll clean it up right away. And I'll replace the bottle," I say, becoming the obedient boy I'd once been in Unity.

"You sure as hell will," Alex says, his face a deep red. "And then you can both start looking for new jobs."

Jimmy's eyes widen. I expect him to defend himself, but he says nothing. He just looks to me. I know I should explain, take the entire blame, tell Alex that Jimmy was not at fault. The obedient boy in me wants to do that, but I can't forget his words about Celeste. *Just another ignorant sister wife.* The anger flickers again. Jimmy's quitting work anyway to go back to school. He doesn't need this job. And without him to pick me up, I have no way to get to work anyway.

"You can take your friggin' job and shove it."

Twelve

I pull the blanket tighter around me and stare numbly at the TV. We have no heat, and ice is beginning to crust around the windowpanes—on the inside. Charlie got busted just after Christmas on drug-trafficking charges. He's in a pretrial detention center, awaiting his day in court. Brent gets occasional work at the local mill, and when he gets paid, he brings home some food and a case or two of beer. But without Charlie's income and with the constant threat of eviction, our little family is drifting apart.

Selig really did leave for the big city, just headed off to the highway one day and stuck out his thumb. A couple of the boys found relatives who gave them work at family operations provided they stay away from Springdale and all its evil temptations. They're also forbidden to visit their family homes, so they've shacked up in a crumbling cabin close to Unity. Those relatives have made it clear that they have no work for me.

It seems there are different degrees of apostate, and I'm the worst kind—the kind that tries to corrupt their pure girls.

I shut off the TV and look around the apartment. It's February, but the Christmas tree still huddles in the corner, the baubles mostly knocked off and broken during an episode of roughhousing. Dirty dishes and takeout trash are scattered on every surface. I pick my way over empty beer cans and discarded clothing. I find a thin jacket in the closet and pull on somebody's left-behind rubber boots, then stomp down the stairs and out onto the frozen sidewalk. The icy wind instantly freezes my nose hairs. I pull up the jacket hood and tuck my hands under my armpits. Head down, I slip and slide all the way to the café where Belle works.

The chimes over the door tinkle when I enter the shop. A blast of warm air hits me. Belle rushes over. "You can't come in," she whispers, looking over her shoulder.

"I have nowhere else to go."

"Bert says you can't just sit in here anymore unless you buy something."

"Then why don't you buy me a hot chocolate?" I lean in to kiss her, but she pushes me away. "Go home, Jon," she says.

"I just need to warm up for a bit."

"Go, Jon." She gives me another shove. "You're going to get me fired."

"Will you come by tonight?" I ask.

She doesn't meet my eyes but shakes her head.

"How about I come to your place then?"

She shakes her head again.

I don't ask why.

After walking around outside a little longer I go to the library and head straight to the computers to see if Craig has sent any more email messages. He hasn't. I don't know why I bother checking. For months he kept writing, urging me to go back to school. I never replied. But it was still nice to know that someone was thinking about me.

I grab my favorite book—*Make Your Own Inuksuk*—and sit in the lounge area, looking at the pictures. It's comfy in the over-stuffed chairs. The light from the window pours in. As I turn the pages, I remember the beach in Unity and building inuksuit with Celeste. The library is warm, and my eyelids get heavy.

A toe lightly kicks my leg, waking me with a start. I sit up, expecting to see a librarian asking me to leave, but it's Wolf. "Fancy meeting you in the library," he says, grinning.

I sit up and stretch, trying to come fully awake. "Why aren't you in school?"

"Pro-D day."

"What day?" I ask, forgetting that I wasn't going to ask questions anymore when I didn't understand something.

"Day off for kids, not teachers."

"And you're spending your day in the library?"

He shrugs. "Not a bad place if you like books."

I yawn. He drops into the armchair across from me but doesn't open his book.

"What've you been up to?" he asks, looking me over.

I comb my fingers through my long hair. When was the last time I washed it? I try to see myself through his eyes. It's not a pretty picture. My chin's raw with zits, and the borrowed clothes I'm wearing don't fit well nor are they clean. "I was working," I tell him. "Building houses, but there's not much construction in the winter." It's not exactly a lie. "How are the girls?"

"The same. Doing a lot of partying, from what I hear."

"Partying?" Maybe they'd invite me along. There've been too many nights when I've had to fall asleep without anything to numb the ugly voices in my head.

"You don't want to party with them," Wolf says, likely reading my expression. "Jailbait."

Jailbait? I don't ask. Now that I'm fully awake, I remember to keep my ignorance to myself.

"So how do you get by?" Wolf asks.

I shrug a shoulder. "Not that well right now. You have any cash I can borrow?" Begging is getting easier. "I'll pay you back next time I get some work."

Wolf shakes his head.

"How about food?"

His eyebrows arch, but he reaches into his pack and tosses me a granola bar.

I rip the wrapper off and eat it in two quick bites. When I look up, he's staring at me. "Maybe my shit's not so bad after all," he says. He shoves his book into his pack and leaves the lounge.

I shiver in my too-thin coat. At exactly three o'clock the school doors burst open, and a swarm of kids pours straight down the stairs and across the school grounds toward after-school activities, jobs or homes. It's too cold for them to linger on the school grounds or hang out at the park as they did in the fall.

It's the third day in a row that I've waited outside the school, hoping to see Crystal coming through the doors. I've chosen a different door to wait at each day, hiding under my hood, hoping not to be recognized. After fifteen minutes I'm about to return to the warmth of the library, but then I see her. As I'd hoped, she's alone as she comes through the door and crosses the playing field. She pulls up her hood as the cold air hits her and walks quickly in my direction.

"Hi, Crystal," I say.

She stops and stares, but I can see from her blank expression that she doesn't immediately recognize me. I push back my hood. "It's me, Jon."

"Oh!" Her eyes widen as she takes in my appearance. "I didn't recognize you."

"How are you?"

"I'm good," she says, still staring at me. "What happened to you, anyway?"

I'm not sure if she's commenting on my appearance or if she really doesn't know why I'm no longer at school. I take a guess. "I quit school. It wasn't working out for me."

"I knew that much. Wolf told us."

I guessed wrong. "I was working," I tell her. "Making great money, but there's been a lull during the winter months."

She nods, still staring wide-eyed. "So what are you doing here?"

"I just came by looking for you. Thought you might like to hang out sometime."

She takes a step back. "I don't know, Jon."

I give her the biggest smile I can muster and step toward her. "Hey, we had fun. Remember chilling during all those lunch hours? And those jokes we played on Wolf?"

She glances around, probably looking for help in case I step any closer to her.

"I bet you like to toke a little," I say. "And do shots. My roomies are legal. I could get you anything you want."

She takes a wide step around me. "Sorry, Jon," she says. "I gotta go."

She scurries away, taking one last look at me over her shoulder. As I trudge back toward the warm library, I catch a glimpse of my reflection in a store window. I stop and stare, shocked. What an idiot. I knew I was a bit scruffy and a little unclean, but the guy in the reflection looks like a homeless, filthy beggar much, much older than I am. Did I really think she'd still flirt with me and get me some pot? What a loser I've become.

I peer into the fridge, hoping that some food has miraculously materialized since the last time I looked. It hasn't.

"It's your turn to stock it," Bruce says from his place on the floor in front of the TV. His voice is muffled by the blanket draped over his head, shrouding his face. "I'm tired of being the sole provider around here."

It's been just the two of us for weeks now. I think about all the food in the kitchen of that last house I worked at—shelves and shelves of it. It would take months for a family to eat it all. A lot of it would likely spoil. I spread ketchup on half of the remaining crust from a loaf of stale bread, mustard on the other half, and join Bruce on the floor.

★   ★   ★

When I'm sure everyone but Taviana will be at school or work, I knock on Abigail's front door. It opens just a crack. Tav peers out. It opens wider.

"Jon?" she asks, as if not recognizing me.

"Who else?" I give her my cheeriest smile. I am such a phony.

"What do you want?"

"Aren't you going to invite me in? It's cold out here."

She hesitates, and for a moment I think she's actually going to turn me away. I watch an internal struggle tug at her face before she pushes the door all the way open. I follow her into the living room.

Nothing has changed. Photos of Abigail's kids cover the walls, and the old couch still faces the TV. Everything is in its place. The carpet looks freshly vacuumed. Was it only eight months ago I first stepped into the room?

Taviana sits in Abigail's armchair, and I settle onto the couch. I run my hand across the cushion. This couch would be much more comfortable than the one I'm currently sleeping on.

"Why are you here?" Taviana asks.

"I just came by to say hi," I tell her.

"It's only taken you five months," she says. "Somehow I don't buy it."

"Seriously, I've missed you. And the others." It's not until I hear my own words that I realize how true they are. A wave of longing washes over me.

"Craig was home at Christmas. He came by to ask where you were."

"You didn't tell him?"

She shakes her head. "It doesn't look like things have worked out so well for you," she says, giving me the once-over. "Jimmy said you looked like crap. He was right."

It hurts, but I don't respond. What is there to say?

"So what are you doing now?"

"Not much. I'll get work in the spring."

Taviana raises an eyebrow. "Not with Alex you won't."

"There are other builders."

"It's a small town, Jon. Word gets around. Alex isn't about to give you a glowing reference."

"Yeah, well, that's my problem. Why are you acting so ticked at me?"

"Jimmy told me what happened."

I've tried to smoke away my shame from that day. Drink it away. "He called Celeste an ignorant sister wife," I mumble, knowing it's really no excuse. I pick at a scab on my chin.

"Who did?"

"Jimmy."

"And that's why you didn't tell Alex what really happened?"

"He could see for himself what really happened."

She cocks her head. "And what was that?"

"Jimmy already told you."

"I want to hear your version."

"I helped myself to some milk and broke a bottle of booze."

"When Jimmy called Celeste an ignorant sister wife," she confirms.

I just nod, and my shame grows with the silence that fills the room.

"It's not too late to call Alex and tell him that."

I can't answer her. It does seem like a simple fix. But basically, I haven't got the balls to call Alex.

"Alex didn't end up firing Jimmy."

"He didn't?"

"No. Once he cooled down he realized it wasn't Jimmy's fault."

That makes me feel a little better.

"But you still need to apologize to them both."

Right. Like that's going to happen. "Did you guys can any of my vegetables?" I ask, anxious to change the subject.

"Is that why you came here? You want some canned vegetables?"

"I grew them."

"In Abigail's yard."

"I built the garden and bought the soil and seeds."

She just stares at me. "I thought for sure you'd come over to apologize to Jimmy," she says.

"You just said he didn't get fired after all."

"But you didn't know that." She's quiet for a moment. "And you knew he'd be at school today." She sighs and then gets up. "Follow me."

She leads the way down the stairs and toward the cold storage room at the far end of the basement. I glance into my old bedroom and see clothes hanging in the closet and shoes on the floor.

"Who's got my old room?" I ask, feeling possessive.

"David."

"David? Jimmy has a new recruit?"

"Not a recruit, Jon. Abigail has given another boy a place to live. His parents kicked him out. Jimmy heard about him and tracked him down. Kind of like what he did for me."

"Is it David Fischer?"

"Yeah."

"He's so young." I remember that David was already prone to pissing off the Prophet at a young age. "Maybe it's better to get them early. He'll have a better chance of catching up."

Taviana just shrugs.

"I wish him luck," I say, remembering the words of the truck driver who dropped me off in Springdale. Someone else I've failed.

Taviana has flicked on the lights in the cold storage room. There are rows of jars on the built-in shelves. She picks up a cardboard box. "Take as many as you can carry."

I line the bottom of the box with jars of tomatoes, beans and pickles. I reach for another jar and peer into it.

"Peaches," she says. "You didn't grow those, but take them anyway." She takes another jar off the shelf and puts it in the box. "Salsa. I remember you liked it."

"You put it on my eggs," I say. "The night I arrived." The night that seems like forever ago.

She studies my face for a moment, and her expression softens. "Yeah." She grabs a second jar and adds it to my box. "Enjoy."

When the box is full, I struggle under its weight up the stairs.

Taviana opens the front door for me. I squeeze by her and then stop. "I never asked about you. How's school working out?"

"Come back when you've got your act together," she says. Her face has hardened again. "And I'll tell you all about it."

She shuts the door behind me.

Thirteen

I'm aware of brightness. It must be morning. My eyes are glued shut, and my head is pounding. Stones poke into my back. A shiver runs through me, and I burrow into my thin sleeping bag, willing myself to return to that blissful state of unconsciousness where nothing matters.

It doesn't work. The fear of being discovered has resurfaced, and I have to figure out where I am.

I force open first my right eye, then my left, but shut them tight again. The sunlight is painfully bright. And I've registered enough of my surroundings to know I'm not in any immediate danger of being discovered.

My sleeping bag is tightly tangled around me, and I can't change positions. Memories from last night begin to rise to the surface, images that are mostly identical to other nights. First there was the discovery of some perfectly good bread and cheese thrown into the Dumpster behind The Village

Table, the restaurant Selig had worked at. He'd given me the heads-up about all the food that gets wasted there. Best-before dates don't mean much when you're hungry.

Then I'd knocked on a few doors, looking for an empty house. It didn't take long to find one. Garbage cans still sitting at the end of driveways in the late afternoon on garbage pick-up day means the owners aren't yet home from work. Gaining access in this small town is usually easy. The trick is to get in and out fast. Sometimes I take electronics and jewelry to sell, stuffing whatever I can into a pillow-case taken off a bed, but last night, judging by this headache, I just took booze.

The sound of rushing water grows louder than the blood pounding in my brain. I open my eyes again. I'm on the beach at the river. The tree splayed out high above me is the same huge weeping willow that I sat under on my first day in Springdale, eleven months ago. Only this time the leaves are still just buds. I have no recollection of finding my way back here last night.

For four weeks I've been sleeping outside, avoiding the authorities. Being a minor with no fixed address, I have to be careful not to get caught, though I don't know where they'd put me if I was. My parents wouldn't take me back, and neither would Abigail. If they put me in foster care, I'd be gone within the day.

Slowly I wriggle out of my sleeping bag and grab the small pack that I've used as a pillow. Everything I own is in it. I rise carefully, knowing that my head may burst with pain if

I stand upright too quickly. I creep deeper into the brush that runs along the river. In a small clearing, I wrap the sleeping bag around my shoulders and squat. I can see the rocky beach and river through the scrub. Later, when it gets warmer, I'll try to wash off in the river, even though the water will be freezing with spring runoff.

The pounding in my head competes with the hunger pangs in my belly, but I close my eyes again and try to sleep off the hangover. There's a long, empty day ahead of me. Brent and I were evicted from the apartment a month ago, and I've been homeless ever since.

When my eyes blink open again, it's warmer. A movement on the beach catches my eye. A lone figure, kneeling, building something with the stones around him. Craig! I leap up. The explosion in my brain nearly knocks me back down. I head toward him but then stop myself. How can I let him see what has become of me? A bum, sleeping on the beach. When I last saw Craig I was still a squeaky-clean polyg who'd never tasted alcohol and who thought drugs were for losers like Brent and Charlie. Was that really me?

I sit back down and watch as Craig puts one last stone on his rock balance. He stretches, scans the beach and then walks in the direction of the park.

I want to run after him, but I don't. Instead I stagger over to his rock balance. It's amazing how he has placed each rock in such a way that the tower doesn't topple over. It seems to defy gravity. A wave of despair presses down on me. I kick the tower as hard as I can and watch the rocks tumble.

What have I become? Life wasn't this bad when I lived in Unity. There were stupid rules, lots of them. The Prophet was full of shit, but I was loved and cared for. I had a family. I even had God, whatever that means. Now I have nothing. I am nothing. And there's no going back.

★   ★   ★

I find myself in the bushes beside the river each day, hoping to see Craig again, but a whole week passes and he doesn't return. Maybe he was only in town for a visit. I should have talked to him. Loneliness and hunger battle for my attention.

Day after day I watch for him, and each day the buds on the tree become a little closer to bursting open. A week after I first saw him, I wake from a light nap, and he's back. This time he's building an inuksuk. I get up and slowly begin to cross the beach.

Hearing the stones crunch, Craig turns. A grin spreads across his face. "I was hoping that if I built an inuksuk you'd come out of hiding," he says. "It worked."

Our eyes meet, and we study each other. He looks clean and fit, and his smile is warm. For a moment I want to flee, but my feet are glued to the ground. Craig steps forward and pulls me in. I stand frozen to the spot, not returning the embrace, but I breathe in the fresh scent of him. I can only imagine how I must smell.

He releases me. "Listen, Jon," he says gently. "My parents are at work today. Why don't you come home with me, and I'll make you something to eat. You can have a shower and use the washing machine if you want."

It's so like Craig. No questions asked, just assistance offered. Blinking back tears, I nod and then follow him along the beach and into town.

★ ★ ★

An hour and a half later I'm at Craig's parents' table, eating a stack of pancakes that he has whipped up for me. I've taken a long, gloriously hot shower, and I've moved my clothes from the washer to the dryer, which purrs in the next room. Craig has given me a pair of sweatpants and a long-sleeved T-shirt, which he says he doesn't need back. He hasn't asked about my life or how things got this way. Instead he tells me stories about living in residence on campus, nasty cafeteria food and a little bit about his classes.

I tilt my head and take a long swallow of milk, remembering, sheepishly, the milk I drank on that last day I worked for Alex.

"How long have you been home?" I ask, finally feeling satisfied. I lean back in the chair and look around at the cluttered kitchen.

"Two weeks now."

"Will you go back to college in the fall?"

He nods. "That's the plan."

"What are you going to do all summer?"

"I lucked out. Mrs. Kennedy has lined me up with a whole list of kids who need some summer tutoring. Right now I'm seeing a few in the afternoons and evenings, until school gets out for the break."

Lucky kids. Learning with Craig was so different from learning in school. If only I could have completed high school that way.

The food and warm shower have made me sleepy, but before I can ask if there's a bed to nap on, he says, "I've seen Celeste, Jon. Her baby is a month old already."

That wakes me up.

"It's a little girl. Her name is Hope."

I cover my face with my hands. I don't want to know this.

"You okay?"

I don't respond. I just let the news sink in.

"She's planning on leaving Unity. She wants my help. And yours."

My hands drop to my lap. "*Now* she plans to leave?" I croak. "*Now?*" I can't help myself. "Why the hell didn't she leave a year ago, before she had to get married and have a friggin' baby?"

Craig doesn't answer immediately. I push back my chair and begin to pace the room.

"I asked her much the same thing," Craig says. "I asked her why she changed her mind. And she said that when she first laid her eyes on her baby girl, she knew she wanted more for her daughter than she'd had for herself. More choices."

I collapse back into the chair. "Where will she go?"

"Abigail has agreed to take them both. Taviana will help out."

The unjustness of this hits me hard. She's going to Abigail's now that I'm gone. "My father will never allow her to leave."

"She's a little worried about how that's all going to go down."

"She should be."

"Jimmy and I are driving out there tomorrow when everyone's in church," he tells me. "She's going to come up with a reason not to attend the service. We're going to pick her up near the beach. Do you want to come with us?"

Yes! I want to scream. Yes! Yes! Yes! For all these months, seeing Celeste was all that I wanted. But now? Everything has changed. I shake my head, staring at my feet.

"She wants to see you," Craig says softly.

"She wants to see the old Jon. Not this one. Besides, when she sees how badly I've failed...it will scare her. She might not leave."

Craig doesn't say anything. He must agree.

The dryer shuts off. "I'll get my things and get on my way."

I pull everything I own out of the dryer and cram it all into my pack—one pair of jeans, a couple pairs of socks with holes in the heels, two pairs of boxer shorts and three T-shirts. Ironically, it's more than I arrived in town with.

Craig isn't in the kitchen when I return. I look around. There are stacks of books on every surface. He must have inherited his love of books from his parents. On a small desk a laptop sits closed, and there are even books stacked on top of it. I pull open the top drawer of the desk. Pens, notepads, paper clips, scissors and a stapler are jumbled together. There is also a heavy gold watch. I glance around the kitchen again, making sure I'm alone. I slide the watch into the pocket of the sweatpants he's given me. Then I pick up my pack and leave through the back door.

Fourteen

I watch a mother and her toddler leave their table in the mall food court, and I quickly sink into the vacated chair before a cleaner clears away the leftover food. I finish the half-eaten hot dog and French fries left on the tray.

I sense the lady at the next table watching me.

I narrow my eyes at her. "What?"

She quickly looks away and begins to gather up her packages, but as she stands to leave, she picks up her own tray and slides it onto my table. Her burger has been carefully cut in two, and one half, untouched, remains on the paper plate. When I look back up, the woman is winding her way out of the food court. I gobble down the burger and sit back, satisfied. The Prophet is so wrong about gentiles. Their kindness always surprises me. He'd brainwashed us, trying to gain our fear and loyalty by making us believe gentiles are evil.

I look for a water fountain on my way out.

The watch on my wrist shows eleven thirty. Craig and Jimmy will be in Unity now. How long before my father discovers that his youngest wife and their daughter have disappeared?

I rub my thumb over the watch's smooth face. It took a while before I figured out that to set the time you have to pull the little button on the side and then wind it to make the watch run. I take it off my wrist and study the engraving on the back again. I can make out the words *With Love* in the center, but the names above and below that have worn off. It must have been a gift from a woman to a man. Craig's mom to his dad? His grandmother to his grandfather? It could even have been a gift between his great-grandparents, judging by how old it looks. To toss a watch like this into a drawer full of pens and paper, well, no one must want it anymore. I'm doing them a favor by finding it a new home.

I was going to take it directly to the pawnshop before stopping at the mall, but I like the way it feels on my wrist. It's so heavy, you can't forget you're wearing it. The person who wore it before me must have had the exact same wrist size. The leather strap is worn thin around the hole where the gold pin pokes through. The numbers on the face are large and black. I've never worn any kind of jewelry. Adornments are discouraged by the Prophet. I might wait a day or two before I make that stop at the pawnshop. That will also give the dealer a little more time to sell the other pieces I've dropped off.

My thoughts return to Celeste. I try to imagine her arrival at Abigail's this afternoon. The ache to see her intensifies.

I could find a place to hide, watch her arrive. She wouldn't have to see me...

I check the watch again. I should have just enough time to get to Abigail's neighborhood and find a secure hiding place.

★ ★ ★

I squat behind a low hedge in a yard across the street from Abigail's. My legs are cramping up, and I know I'm in full view if anyone's home in the house behind me, but it's the best place I could find to hide.

The minutes tick slowly past. I shift my weight from one foot to the other. They should have arrived by now. Did they get caught? Did Celeste change her mind? So many things could have gone wrong.

Finally I hear Jimmy's pickup coming down the narrow road. I part the hedge's thick branches to watch as he parks at the curb. Immediately Abigail's front door bursts open, and both Abigail and Taviana rush into the yard. Matthew and David appear in the doorway behind them.

Jimmy jumps out of the truck and leans into the cab for something. A moment later he's cradling a baby in his arms. My baby sister.

Craig climbs out of the passenger side and then she's there, standing beside him, her ankle-length skirt and long-sleeved, chin-high blouse so familiar yet so out of place at the same time. It takes all the willpower I have to remain in my hiding place and not run over to her.

"Celeste!" Taviana shrieks. She rushes around the front of the truck to embrace her old friend. They hold each other for a long moment, and I can tell from the way Celeste's shoulders shake that she's crying.

Jimmy has passed the baby to Abigail and is helping Craig lift shopping bags out of the bed of the pickup. They must have stopped to pick up baby supplies. Celeste wouldn't have been able to pack anything.

There's a wail from the baby. Celeste pulls herself away from Taviana to take her from Abigail. As she bounces the baby, introductions are made, and then everyone begins to move toward the house.

Suddenly hands clamp onto my shoulders. I lurch to my feet. I struggle to run, but I'm overpowered by someone taller and heavier than me. "What do you think you're doing?" the big man asks, his voice booming.

I look up. Abigail, Jimmy and Craig have heard the man's voice and are watching what's happening. Celeste has already gone into the house with Taviana.

"Jon?" Abigail asks. She walks across the street. Craig and Jimmy trail her. I twist to release myself from the man's grip, but he's got my arms pinned behind me now. Abigail asks, "What are you doing here?" As soon as the words are out of her mouth, a look of understanding crosses her face. "Oh. You knew Celeste was arriving."

I don't meet her eyes or acknowledge her words.

"You know this punk?" the man asks. "He's been hiding

behind my hedge, behaving suspiciously. Don't tell me this is one of your Lost Boys, Abigail."

"Yes, he is," she says uncertainly.

"I told you not to run a halfway house in our neighborhood," the man says, gripping my arms even tighter. I wince in pain. "You go around acting like Mother Teresa while these damaged polygs turn into hooligans. And worse. I've said it before: I want your little operation shut down. I'm going back to city council about this."

No one says anything for a moment.

"So why were you hiding behind the hedge anyway?" the man asks, still holding my arms.

"I was just…just waiting for them to get home."

"Waiting for *whom* to get home?"

I cock my head toward Jimmy and Craig, who stand quietly beside Abigail.

"Then why didn't you wait over there?"

My mouth opens, but I can't come up with an answer.

"Did you want to surprise Celeste?" Craig asks.

All heads turn to look at him. I can only nod, but I'm intensely grateful.

"Who is Celeste?" the man asks.

"She's an old friend of Jon's," Craig says. "She's just arrived for a visit."

"And you are?" the man asks Craig. "You don't look like you come from Unity."

"I'm Jon's tutor," Craig says. "You can let go of his arms."

The man shifts his grip to the nape of my neck. I shake out my arms and straighten the watch, but then I remember where it came from. It's too late. I glance at Craig. He's staring at it, frowning. He looks up, and our eyes lock. I wait for him to bust me, but he doesn't say anything.

The neighbor gives Abigail one last glare. "Quit harboring these runaways," he says. He releases my neck and gives my back a hard push. He stomps back to his house.

I look toward Abigail's house. Two figures are standing in her living room, watching us. Before anyone can say anything, I turn and run down the street.

★ ★ ★

"I've brought you a sandwich."

I can hear the voice, but it's coming from far away.

"Come on, Jon. Wake up." A toe pokes me in the ribs.

Craig. I try to open my eyes, but it is just too bright. I struggle to say *go away*, but my throat is so dry that only a croak comes out.

I have no idea where I am. Last night is a complete blank. Most of the last week is fuzzy. I'd be better off dead. Maybe one of these mornings I just won't wake up. That would be a blessing.

Drips of water hit my forehead. I force my eyes open and see Craig holding a water bottle over me. Another drop of water splashes my face. "What the…!" I try to roll over, away from him, but sharp stones stab me in the back. "Go away," I repeat, clearer this time.

"I have chocolate chip cookies too," Craig says.

I struggle to sit up. "What do you want?"

"Celeste needs you," he says, passing me a sub sandwich. It's fully loaded with meats, cheeses and vegetables.

I grab it and take huge bites. I have no idea when I last ate. My sole objective has been to find booze, which keeps me blissfully unaware of anything else. When the sandwich is gone, Craig hands me the bottle of water. I drink the whole thing without stopping for air.

I lie back down on a tarp that I acquired from who knows where. As I become more alert I also become less numb. The shame returns. I need to find more booze.

"Celeste needs your help," Craig repeats.

I stare up at him. "What kind of help?"

"Your father keeps calling Abigail's, insisting Celeste return to Unity."

"Well, duh. What did she expect?" I squeeze my eyes shut again.

"He also wants to know where you are."

My eyes pop open. "Did you tell him?"

"No."

That's a relief. I really need a drink. I glance around for my backpack. Maybe there's a bottle in it.

"He hasn't forced her to return yet," Craig says. "He claims he's worried about her safety."

The food and the water have reached my bloodstream, and I feel sleepy again. I close my eyes. "Why are you telling me?" I murmur.

"We figure that if he knew you were caring for her and Hope, he might consider leaving them alone, letting them stay. He trusts you, and he admits he knew how unhappy Celeste has been."

I let this sink in. "Well, as you can see, I can't even take care of myself, let alone her and her baby."

"Jon, listen to me." He sounds uncharacteristically irritated.

I push my long, filthy hair away from my face and force myself to sit up again. "I'm listening."

"There are lots of us who want to help Celeste, but your father doesn't know us. He says he needs to speak with you. You just have to convince him that she'll be okay."

I try to laugh but end up in a coughing fit. "Do you still think he's going to feel that way after he sees me?"

"Come to my house. We'll get you cleaned up, back on track."

"Good luck with that." I flop down again and roll over so my back is toward Craig. I close my eyes, but my head is pounding hard. Craig doesn't say anything else, but I feel his presence. I try to wait him out, hoping he'll just leave, but he doesn't. What's the matter with him? Can't he see that I'm a mess? I can't help Celeste.

But I remember Craig's house. The warm shower, the cozy kitchen. The food. Maybe just for a few days....

With a start, I remember the watch. I glance at my wrist, but, of course, I've pawned it. I needed booze. Craig hasn't mentioned it. He knows I stole it, yet he's still inviting me back. Is he crazy?

Slowly, painfully, I push myself up again. "Did you say you had cookies?"

He takes a container of homemade cookies out of his pack. I help myself to one, then another, and another until they're all gone. I can't remember food ever tasting so good.

Fifteen

For twenty-four hours I do nothing but eat and sleep. Craig gives me a stack of his clothes and throws out all the ones I owned. His parents were kind when Craig introduced us. They told me to make myself at home.

I have.

On the second morning I find Craig puttering in the kitchen.

"How are you feeling today?" he asks when I sit at the table. He slides an omelet in front of me.

I tuck right in. "Almost human."

Craig starts cracking more eggs into a bowl. "That's good." He dices peppers and onion, then grates cheese.

"Where did you learn to cook like this?"

He smiles as he beats the eggs. "You've forgotten that it's only in Unity that the kitchen is out-of-bounds for men. I've been cooking since I was a little kid." He pours the egg mixture into a hot pan. "So," he says. "It's time for us to talk."

My mood plunges. I don't respond but instead concentrate on my food. This may be my last good meal for a while.

"The idea was to get you cleaned up, back on track, and help Celeste out, right?" He transfers the omelet onto a plate and joins me at the table. "Step one is complete. We've cleaned you up. Now we need to get you back on track."

I watch him eat. "And how are we going to do that?"

He glances up. "I think you have to figure that part out for yourself. In the meantime, your father is waiting to talk to you."

"And what do you expect me to say to him?" I can feel the anger bubbling up. "That I live on the street, I steal for a living, and I'm a high-school dropout. But sure, I'll help Celeste out."

"It doesn't have to be that way."

"Yeah, right." I look around at the family pictures hanging on the walls, at the open cupboards stocked with food. Craig's parents even let him take a gap year to "find himself," as he put it, after high school. A year to figure out what he wanted to do with his life. It was at the end of that year that he began tutoring me.

I used to have a home too. But I chose to give it up.

"You can get a job," he says. "You can find a place to live. You can even return to school."

"No one's going to hire a homeless high-school dropout. Besides, I burned all my bridges in the construction industry. I have no references."

"Then get references."

"Maybe you didn't hear. Alex fired me. He was my only hope for a reference."

"I heard," he says quietly. "And I think you could rebuild those bridges."

"Easy for you to say."

He shrugs. "I didn't say it was going to be easy, but sleeping on the beach didn't look too…too easy either."

He's right. After a couple of nights on a soft bed, the thought of sleeping on the beach again has no appeal. And having a clear head for the last couple of days—for those few hours I've been awake anyway—has been kind of nice too.

"What do you suggest I do?"

"Apologize to Alex and Jimmy." Craig says it like it's the simplest thing in the world.

I slide lower in my chair. "It's way too late for that."

"It's never too late. And even if Alex won't hire you again, it's the right thing to do."

"Yeah, but your *right thing* won't get me a job." I get up and put my dishes in the dishwasher. "How's she doing anyway?"

"Celeste? Well, it's been an adjustment for her. Not only does she have to get used to living outside Unity, but she's also learning how to be a mother, and she's just a girl herself."

"Lots of sixteen-year-old girls in Unity have babies," I tell him. "Maybe most of them." I fill the sink and put the frying pan into the soapy water. As I scrub at the stuck-on omelet I realize he's trying to tell me that Celeste has it harder than I did. That irritates me.

"I think she expected you to be here for her," Craig adds, almost under his breath.

My mind returns to that last morning in Unity, when I begged her to come with me. I'd promised her we'd be together, that we'd get an education and make the kind of life for ourselves that we could never have there.

I place the pan on the drainboard and rinse off the knives. Now she's here, but with a baby. My half sister. And I've turned into a bum, all my plans sunk into a deep, dark hole.

"Is Abigail insisting that she finish high school too?"

Craig nods.

"I don't know how she'll do that with a child to look after." I wipe the counters and return to the table. "It might be better if she goes back," I tell him. I mean it.

"Too late," he says. "She cut her hair, she's wearing jeans, and she's talking about getting a tattoo."

"Are you kidding me?"

He laughs. "Only about the tattoo." His face grows serious again. "She deserves a chance, Jon. All you have to do is convince your father that she's safe, so he can set her free. You know that the rest of us will take care of her." He shakes his head. "He's struggling too. The Prophet's furious that he's not physically dragging her back to Unity. He's lost face in the community. At least if he knows that she'll be safe here, he can stop worrying about that."

I think about my father. He is a good guy. Fair. Kind. I just couldn't share his religious beliefs. But I really miss him.

I even feel for him, dealing with the Prophet right now. It's got to be hard.

"And Jon?" he says.

I meet his eyes.

"She'd like to see you. Today, if possible. Will you do that for her?"

I fold my hands in my lap and notice my fingernails. They're clean. I trimmed them for the first time in months. Same with my toenails. It feels good.

Craig is watching me closely. The thought of seeing Celeste terrifies me, but I'd rather it be now than when I'm back on the street, dirty, hungry and probably drunk or high. I nod.

★ ★ ★

Craig leads a girl across the park toward the picnic table where I'm waiting. The girl is pushing a baby carriage. At first I wonder who she is. He was supposed to bring Celeste, but then I realize this *is* her. She's completely transformed. With her shoulder-length hair, cutoff jeans, T-shirt and sandals, she looks like any other pretty Springdale teenager. I stand as they approach the table.

"Hi, Jon," Celeste says. Our eyes meet for a brief moment, and then we both look away.

It disturbs me to see her like this, her legs exposed, her hair framing her face. It's fine for the girls out here, but not for my Celeste. I realize with a start that there's still some of the polygamist living inside me. But something stirs at the sound of her voice. It *is* her.

I clear my throat. "I hardly recognized you," I stammer.

"You look different too," she says. "You've grown taller, and your hair…"

"Oh, yeah, I haven't cut it for a while." I give my ponytail a quick yank. "You should have seen it when I dyed it orange."

"You did?"

"Yup."

"I'll let you two get caught up," Craig says. "I'll be back in a little while. Is that okay?" He directs the question to Celeste.

She hesitates for a moment, then says, "Yeah, sure. See you in a bit."

Craig glances into the buggy, adjusts the baby's blanket and then heads back the way he came.

"Why don't we sit down?" I suggest.

We sink onto the wooden bench. Celeste keeps her hand on the carriage's handle, gently bouncing the baby. I notice the polish on her fingernails. That's new too.

The last time I was with Celeste was the day in the hospital waiting room, when her mom was sick and we fell into each other's arms and kissed as if our lives depended on it. For almost a year now, I've fantasized about another meeting like that, but clearly that's not going to happen today.

"So how is my dad and, well, everyone else?"

"Everyone's fine. They weren't allowed to talk about it, but I know the kids really missed you. And your mom, she…"

She pauses, choosing her words carefully. "She always seemed sad, and she never really warmed to me."

I brace myself against a wave of homesickness as I think about my mom and all my brothers and sisters. "I'm sure she loves you, but it's just—"

"Yeah. I know."

There's no point in stating the obvious—that if we hadn't been secretly meeting, I might not have had to leave so soon, and Celeste certainly wouldn't have been married to my father.

The baby begins to fuss in the carriage, and Celeste rocks it a little harder, but the baby becomes even more agitated. She reaches in and lifts her out. The baby stops fussing immediately, and her blue eyes focus on me. I'm shocked at the family resemblance. She could be any one of my other little sisters.

"Meet Hope," Celeste says, handing the infant to me.

Hope stares at me, wide-eyed. It dawns on me that this may be the only sister I will ever see again. A surge of emotion threatens to unglue me, so I quickly hand her back.

The baby starts to fuss again. "Do you mind if I feed her?" Celeste asks shyly.

"Of course not. Go ahead."

Celeste reaches into the buggy for a light blanket, and I look away as she settles the baby at her breast with the blanket draped over her shoulder for modesty.

"A lot has changed in the last year," she says.

"That's for sure."

"I'm sorry it didn't work out for you at Abigail's."

"Nothing has really worked out for me."

I can feel her glance at me, but she doesn't respond. We sit quietly for a moment, watching small children playing on the playground and a dog chasing a ball. Spring has arrived, and everyone has headed outdoors to enjoy the warm sunshine.

"Do you regret leaving Unity?" Celeste asks.

I ponder her question. "I have days," I tell her. "I really miss my family. And I really missed you." We exchange a quick glance. "But I was really unhappy there too. I have a better chance of finding my way here."

Listen to me, giving her this fake pep talk. I give my head a little shake.

"I hope it works out for me," she says. She pulls the baby out from under the blanket. "I have Hope to think about too."

I take my little sister, put her on my shoulder and begin to pat her. It comes back to me easily. I enjoy the warmth of her little body as she nestles into my neck. I've had lots of experience with babies.

"You know," I say, watching Craig walk across the park toward us, "I think you're going to be just fine."

It's almost exactly a year since I first arrived in Springdale and tasted salsa for the first time in Abigail's living room. I'm in the living room again, only this time I'm waiting for my father to arrive. Abigail is in her armchair, Craig is waiting at the window, and Celeste and I sit beside each other on the couch. Hope is sleeping in Celeste's arms. We thought of including Taviana but decided my father might not see her as a good role model.

We've agreed to stick to the truth as much as possible. Abigail won't tolerate lies. But we've also agreed to spare my father the details of my life that he wouldn't want to hear.

Celeste thought things might go better if I cut my hair, so Craig took me to a local barber. I can always grow it out again. She's not wearing the dress she arrived in, but she is fully covered in long pants and a sweater buttoned to the neck.

Craig has tried to keep a patter of small talk going while we wait, but we're all distracted. Now we just stare at the sleeping baby. Abigail knits. My left foot keeps twitching. If I don't convince my father to leave Celeste here, they'll all be disappointed in me. I'll lose this second chance I've been given to be with Celeste. I feel like I might explode from the pressure. Just seeing my dad again, after all this time...

I could use a drink. Something strong.

Eventually a truck pulls up outside Abigail's house. I take a deep breath and let it out slowly. I sense Celeste stiffening. She's pale. There are dark circles under her eyes. She looks at me, frightened. I just nod and try to look more confident than I feel. I have to do this for her. Craig's right. She deserves a chance. Just because I failed doesn't mean she will too.

My father steps out of the truck and glances toward the house. He looks older than I remember and a little stooped. This meeting is probably as hard for him as it is for me.

Abigail gets up and opens the front door. The sound of his voice as he greets her spins me back to my childhood, when that same voice caused a pack of small children to run across the house toward him when he returned home at the end of each day. He was the fun parent, unlike the tired, overworked moms.

I stand and step toward the door. When my father sees me, his eyes well up with tears. "Jon."

"Hi, Dad."

We stare at each other for a moment. A million unspoken thoughts hang in the air between us. Then he steps toward me and folds me in a warm embrace. "I've missed you, son," he says. His words take me by surprise. According to the laws of his religion, I am no longer his son. In fact, I don't even exist.

I swallow the boulder-sized lump in my throat. "I've missed you too."

Eventually we release each other, and I introduce him to Craig. When my father sees Celeste he looks surprised. Her haircut has really changed her appearance. He hesitates and his eyes brim with tears again. "Celeste," he says. "It's good to see you."

She nods, but I note she doesn't make eye contact with him.

In that moment I'm hit with an image of them together in bed, and my stomach clenches. I've put it out of my mind until now, but Hope is his child, after all. It makes me sick. My year in Springdale has shown me that teenage girls are not meant to be married to men as old as their own fathers. It's not the natural order of things. I suddenly see my father through different eyes. Why did he never question the religious practices in Unity?

Abigail directs him to an empty chair. His eyes rest on Hope, still cradled in Celeste's arms and sleeping peacefully. "How is she doing?"

"Good. Starting to smile a little."

My father nods. He doesn't ask to hold her. I try to remember how many children he has now. Eighteen? Nineteen? Another sister wife had a baby after I left, but I've lost count.

"So," my father says, clearing his throat. "The Prophet has directed me to bring you home, Celeste. You are my wife and belong with my family. Hope is my daughter."

No one responds. I've forgotten my well-rehearsed lines. Craig comes to my rescue.

"As you know, sir, Jon plans to watch over Celeste."

Thank you, Craig.

"And Hope too, of course," he adds.

I can only nod. I feel completely inadequate to take care of anything.

"Our community is a better fit for Celeste," Craig continues. "She would never be happy if she returned to Unity. I really hope you will put her needs first and choose what is best for her."

Abigail jumps in. "Celeste and Hope will have a stable home here," she says. "I have strict rules that Celeste has agreed to follow. I will support her as best as I can, and the others have all offered to help as well, with babysitting and tutoring. You can rest assured that she will be well taken care of."

"It's true, Dad," I say, finally finding my voice. "Everyone is ready to help her. She'll be okay."

I can feel him looking at me, but I can't meet his eyes.

"And how have *you* fared here, son?"

In that moment I know that the truth about my failure has reached my family back home. I glance at Craig and then at Abigail for help, but they only nod encouragingly. "I won't lie to you, Dad. It hasn't always been easy. Especially school. But I've learned from my mistakes and can help make sure that Celeste doesn't make the same ones. And having Hope will be an extra incentive for her to succeed."

I promised Abigail I wouldn't lie, but have I really learned anything from my mistakes?

My father sighs. "This is really difficult for me," he says. "I want to live by the rules of my faith, which tell me to take Celeste home. She will be cared for and supported there just as much as she will be here. And it's not just me who wants you back, Celeste," he says, looking directly at her. "You have caused suffering to your parents and your brothers and sisters, as well as to all my other wives and children."

I was hoping he wouldn't bring up Celeste's family. That's her weakness, what kept her from leaving Unity with me a year ago. I glance at her, but she simply looks at the floor.

"I hear that your sister, Rebecca, has been especially hurt by your...your choices," he says.

Rebecca is Celeste's little sister, whom she was particularly close to. It's a low blow.

"You know you'll never see any of them again, right?" It's like the lid slamming on the coffin. I can almost hear the nails being hammered in.

Celeste still doesn't say anything, but her hands are trembling, and she squeezes Hope tighter. I'm disgusted with my father, using this tactic to change Celeste's mind. My respect for him crumbles.

Celeste wipes her nose with the back of her hand. Abigail gets up and passes her a box of tissues. She takes a few wipes at her eyes. Right now I have no idea what decision she'll make. Coming into this meeting I was sure she would stay. I'm no longer so sure. Without any thought of the consequences, I move closer to her and throw my arm around her shoulder, pulling her in. She looks surprised, then looks up at me, grateful.

Hope begins to squirm. Abigail takes her from Celeste. She sways, back and forth. I can see how much she loves having a baby in her arms again.

"This…this incident," my father says, "will be forgiven, Celeste. I promise you that no one will refer to it after you return home."

Celeste shrinks lower under my arm. I'm losing her. I remember how in the hospital she desperately wanted to stay in Springdale with me, but the pull of her family was too much. It's happening again.

I meet Craig's eyes. He looks as worried as I feel.

"Dad," I say, removing my arm from Celeste's shoulder and sitting up taller, "Celeste wouldn't have made the brave decision to leave Unity if she didn't know it was the best thing for her and for Hope. Returning would be a step backward." I shift so I can look into Celeste's face. There are tears streaming down her cheeks. I put my fingers under her chin, lifting her face so she can look back at me. "Remember why you decided to leave Unity, Celeste? It was for Hope, wasn't it? So she could have more choices in her life than you did. Don't you still want that for her?"

As she looks back at me, something changes in her expression. Her jaw clenches. She closes her eyes and takes a deep breath. The tension in the room is thick. I hold my own breath. Hope suddenly cries out, and we all jump.

"I'm staying here, Martin," Celeste tells my father. There's a collective *whoosh* as the air starts moving again.

I reach out to hold Celeste, and she clings fiercely to me, a life preserver.

My father hasn't moved. His head hangs down. He stares at his clasped hands. No one says anything. Finally he looks up and meets my eyes. "I'm counting on you, Jon, to keep them both safe."

Without thinking, I blurt out the words. "You can count on me, Dad."

I sense the look that passes between Craig and Abigail. Neither of them believes me. I'm not sure I do either, but I've kept my word to them. I've done everything I can to keep Celeste here.

My father gets up and steps over to Abigail, who is still holding Hope. He stares down at her for a moment and then strokes her cheek with one finger. Hope looks at him with her huge blue eyes. Then he turns and heads to the door. I follow him, surprised that he's given in so easily. Perhaps he always knew he'd be leaving without her but had to put up a fight for appearances. I follow him out to his truck, feeling sad even after all this. He's still the father I once loved with all my heart. Now I'm never going to see him again.

"You know, Jon," he says, "a little part of me respects both you and Celeste."

"You're kidding." I can't hide my surprise.

"No, really. Sometimes I question the Prophet too, but I never say anything." He climbs into his truck, shuts the door and rolls down the window. "I love you, son."

He rolls the window back up and pulls away from the curb. I watch until he's around the corner.

Back in the house, Celeste is feeding Hope, and Craig is now sitting on the couch beside her. I find Abigail emptying the dishwasher in the kitchen. "I was proud of you today, Jon," she says. "You really stood up for Celeste."

It feels weird to hear that anyone could be proud of me. Especially her. "Do you know where I can find Jimmy?" I ask.

She looks at the clock on the wall. "He should be home from school in about half an hour. How come?"

I can't meet her eyes. "I have some apologizing to do."

"Oh." She turns back to the dishwasher. "You're welcome to stay and wait for him."

"Thanks." I watch her for a moment, undecided. Then I bite the bullet. "Would you mind if I clean up the garden?"

"No. I wouldn't mind."

"And if it's okay with you, maybe I'll plant vegetables again. I wouldn't need to come into the house—I'd just enter from the lane."

She joins me at the window and looks into the backyard. "That would be really nice, Jon."

Epilogue

Today is my day to take care of Hope. I've watched her every Saturday for almost five years now, ever since Celeste decided to stay in Springdale.

Her little face is peering out the living room window, watching for me. As soon as I pull up in front of Abigail's house, she rushes out the front door, runs across the lawn and is standing beside the car door before I can even climb out. "Jon!" she shouts as I pick her up and twirl her around. Then I pull her into a tight hug, breathing her in, my heart softening. My beautiful little sister.

She squirms, and I let her down. "Hi, Lauren," she says, giving a cheerful wave.to the girl climbing out of the passenger seat. Lauren smiles and waves back.

"What are we doing today?" Hope asks.

I squat so we're face-to-face. "Well, first I'm taking you to Hope House with me. I've got to get some work done before the big celebration tomorrow, but Lauren has packed a bag of games for you and her to play. She's also packed a picnic, with watermelon for dessert."

"Yum!" Hope claps her hands. "Will Jimmy be there?"

"Yep. And if I can get everything done this morning, we'll get ice cream and go to the park this afternoon."

"Hope House! Hope House!" She begins to march around my car, chanting the name of the center that has been named for her. Hearing it always gets her going.

Celeste walks toward us with Hope's little backpack and booster seat. "Hey," I say, taking them from her with one hand and hugging her with my other. As always, a twinge of sadness tugs at me. I think back to those days when she first arrived at Abigail's, and how hard we tried to resume our relationship. We'd meet on the beach and build inuksuit, like we used to in Unity, only now we didn't have to do it on the sly. Hope would sleep under the trees in her baby carriage.

But where we used to talk endlessly about finding a way to be together, our conversations had stumbled, neither of us willing to share much about the year we were apart. It was apparent from the start that something had shifted between us. We were shy with each other, awkward. Both of us had experienced life in ways that had changed us. We'd both lost our innocence but in different ways.

Still, I was fiercely drawn to her, despite the changes I could see, and I knew that she still wanted to be with me. It had taken a few weeks, but I'd finally found the courage to coax her into the privacy of the bushes, where we lay down, like before, and I began to kiss her. It took a few moments, but slowly the tension left her body and she responded, kissing me back. It was everything I'd been dreaming of for that whole wretched year.

And then Hope had awoken with a howl, an abrupt reminder to me that Celeste had been my father's wife, that she'd had sex with him. Hope was my sister.

In the end, I just couldn't get past that. Celeste didn't question why I never kissed her again. I'd catch her watching me, but I think she felt strange about it too. Technically, I was now her stepson. The weird nature of our polygamous sect meant that our being together was a kind of incest. And, of course, we were young. She was barely sixteen and I was only eighteen, even though months of living on the street had made me grow up quickly.

"Hey, Celeste," Lauren greets her. "Studying today?"

"No," she says. "I picked up a shift at the bistro. I'll study tonight, after Hope's asleep."

"Are you looking forward to the celebration tomorrow?"

"Yeah! Totally."

"What are you going to wear?"

Before Celeste can answer, I hand her the booster seat. "Could you strap Hope in for me?" I ask. "I need to water the vegetables while I'm here."

I jog around to the back of the house and check my garden. Carrot greens are already poking up through the rich soil.

I was never invited to live at Abigail's again, but I've been helping her out by growing vegetables each year. I'll do the same at Hope House, and I'll continue to deliver a weekly basket to the man across the street, the man whose hedge I hid behind the day Celeste arrived. Taviana still drops off homemade muffins to him during the winter months. Our peace offering seems to be working. Abigail's safe home for young polygs hasn't been shut down yet.

After spraying water on the raised beds, I jog back to the front yard, give Celeste another quick hug and then climb into my little car.

"Bye, Mommy!" Hope waves from the backseat as I pull away. Through the rearview mirror I see Celeste waving back.

Lauren, my girlfriend for the past three years, has five younger siblings, and she often brings some of their toys to share with Hope. Now she pushes a CD into the car's ancient player and the two of them start singing along with Bobs & LoLo.

It was probably Lauren's large family that really sealed our relationship. Being among all those little brothers and sisters almost felt like being back home. I guess her parents were willing to see past my obvious flaws and allow Lauren to date me because of the way I settled into the family as if it were my own.

When we reach Hope House, Lauren and I gather up the bags of toys and food while Hope scampers ahead of us. Hope House has been Jimmy's project for the past three years. It started as a simple college assignment. Jimmy wrote about an imaginary safe house for girls who wanted to leave Unity. His focus had been on the kinds of support that girls need to get used to their new lives. Celeste was his main resource for the project. His teacher really liked his concept and encouraged him to turn the idea into reality.

When Alex heard about it, he began scouting around for an actual house. He found one, old and abandoned, and then he and Abigail began fundraising for renovations. It's been a labor of love for many of us. We all pitch in between work, school and helping care for Hope. Hope will be one of the first occupants, with Celeste. Abigail will move in too, when she's needed, and then Alex will take on the responsibilities at Abigail's and watch over the boys who continue to arrive each year.

The big question is whether other girls like Celeste will be brave enough to escape. That's where Taviana has helped out, slipping into Unity dressed in Celeste's old dress and staying away from the older generation. She reconnects with the girls she knew during the months she lived there, finding them on the playground with their small children or out hanging clothes on lines or working in their gardens. Jimmy wants to entice the girls away before they are assigned to a marriage. He coached Taviana to plant in them the seed of hope for a better future, like he did with us boys, but it's more likely that Hope House will be a refuge for young polygamist wives and mothers. Underage girls who leave create a whole other set of problems, such as kidnapping charges. Parents don't often come after the Lost Boys, but the girls are another matter. Still, if the young mothers know that they have a place to run to, they may be more willing to leave.

I'd fantasized about getting Celeste's little sister Rebecca out as a way to get back at Dad for using her to try to lure Celeste back to Unity. Jimmy had to convince me that she's still way too young. Maybe someday. At least now there is somewhere for her and all my little sisters to come to. Abigail holds out hope for her granddaughters.

As Lauren and I approach the house I notice a strange object on the porch. A bright orange tarp is draped over a shape taller than me and wider. I walk toward it, but Lauren tugs my hand, pulling me back.

"What is it?" I ask. Obviously she knows something I don't.

"A surprise," she says. "You'll find out tomorrow."

I look at her for a moment, wondering how she can know something about this project that I don't. I'm tempted to pull my hand free and run over to investigate, but she steps in front of me and gets up on her tippy-toes to give me a kiss. It's a lingering one, and I forget about the unidentified object for a moment.

"Hey, you two." Alex's voice draws me back to the present. He's standing at the door, watching us. "You're here to work."

"Sorry, Alex," Lauren says. "He was about to go uncover the you-know-what."

"Ah, good work, Lauren. Jimmy was supposed to keep him away from it. Come this way and check things out, Jon."

I follow him into the house. It's a beehive of activity. There's a plumber working under the kitchen sink, an electrician in the utility room and a couple of friends painting interior walls. In the week since I was last here, the donated furniture has been delivered and put into place.

"How does it look?" Alex asks.

"Amazing!"

I wander around, admiring the donated couches and chairs. In the kitchen I open the cupboard doors and find the shelves fully stocked with dishes and cooking utensils that Abigail and Taviana purchased from secondhand stores.

Down the hall, the four small bedrooms each have beds and nightstands. Cushions and extra blankets add an inviting touch. I suspect the three additional bedrooms in the basement look much the same, though it may be a while before all the rooms are occupied, if they ever are. This is still a project based on faith, as well as on hope.

"Where shall I start?" I ask Alex once Lauren and Hope have settled in the living room to play board games.

My relationship with Alex, though strained after I first apologized, has been patched up, and I'm now a supervisor in his company. He hired me back on the condition that I give up all drugs and alcohol. That wasn't too difficult once I had purpose in my life again—the promise I made to my father. Alex then surprised me by offering me a room in his home for minimal rent.

At first I was shocked by his generosity and unable to accept this kindness. After what I'd done, how could he trust me again? But I did eventually move out of Craig's parents' house and into a spare bedroom at Alex's place, and I stayed there until I could afford to rent a basement suite with a carpenter friend.

Jimmy was much slower to accept my apology, and I don't blame him. I'd been such an ass. When I found out about his Hope House project, which was just an idea on paper then, I felt even worse. He came from the same place that I did, but instead of letting his past ruin him, as I had been doing, he was trying to make a difference. The longer it took for him to accept my apology, the worse I felt. I would likely have ended up on the street again except that two things happened, almost simultaneously.

The first was that I tried to recover the watch I'd stolen from Craig's house.

"Sorry, it's been sold," the pawn dealer said.

If I could have put my hands on a bottle that day, I would have guzzled the whole thing. As it was, I'd been sober for a few weeks. The realization of what I'd done hit hard. That wasn't any old watch—it was a family treasure, inscribed with love.

While I was contemplating my next move, possibly stealing something else in order to buy drugs to numb the guilt, the second thing happened. Celeste called and asked me to watch Hope for her. She had to meet with Mrs. Kennedy, the school counselor, and then she had a couple of job interviews. I was still living at Craig's at that point, doing nothing. She brought Hope to me. My plan had been to watch her for that one day, then pack up my few belongings and hit the streets again. To hell with what I'd told my father.

Hope was asleep in her carriage when Celeste dropped her off. I remained in my chair, staring into space, bracing myself for my return to street life. When Hope began to fuss, I lifted her out of the carriage and plugged a baby bottle into her mouth.

She studied me for the entire time it took her to drink that bottle.

I tried to see myself through her eyes. She was too unaware of the world to know that I was a complete failure. A thief. A bum. All she saw was her oldest brother. Light-brown hair. Blue eyes. Metal stud in one earlobe.

We locked eyes and continued to stare at each other. I felt that she was deciding whether she could trust me to keep her safe, warm and dry. When she finished sucking, I tugged the bottle out of her mouth, and her little face broke into a bright, toothless smile. I'd passed the test. I propped her on my knee and began to pat her back. In that moment I realized Hope had been seeing *me*, not the bum who'd given up on himself, and I wanted to be the big brother she could count on.

I held her for the rest of that day, even when she fell back to sleep, and continued to study her peaceful face. I could feel a sense of protectiveness swell in me. I had to keep Hope safe from harm. I knew Celeste had Abigail, Taviana and the other boys to help her, but this was my little sister. I wanted to be someone she could be proud of.

When Craig returned that afternoon, after Celeste had collected Hope, I approached him immediately, before my newfound resolve could evaporate.

"About that watch," I said. "The one I stole from your family."

He nodded and waited for me to continue.

"I took it to a pawnshop. I needed the money."

He remained quiet.

I took a deep breath and let it pour out. "I know now how stupid that was. I regret it. I went to the pawnshop to get it back, but it had been sold." I crumpled into the nearest chair. "I am so sorry. I don't know why you welcomed me back here, knowing what I did."

Eventually Craig spoke. "Jon?"

I met his eyes.

He pulled up his sleeve, and there was the watch. On his wrist.

"You bought it from the pawnshop?" I asked.

He nodded.

"How did you know where it was?"

"Lucky guess."

"Why didn't you say anything?"

"I knew you'd eventually want to talk about it. But I didn't want to push you before you were ready."

I stared at him. "How did you know I wouldn't steal something else?"

There was a long pause. "I didn't know for sure, but I decided to trust you."

I blinked back tears. For months I'd been telling myself that the world was conspiring against me, that none of what had happened to me was my fault. It was the Prophet's fault.

My father's fault. Even Abigail's and Jimmy's faults. But now I'd found out that Craig chose to trust me. Now I had an opportunity for a fresh start with Hope. I could show her who I really was.

"I'll pay you back. I promise."

"I know."

Shortly after that I moved into Alex's home. Jimmy began to soften. We worked together over the summer, and he eventually started talking to me again. He even apologized for calling Celeste an ignorant sister wife. He knew her by then and felt bad that he'd called her that. I used Alex's computer to sign up for online courses to complete my high-school diploma. It's taken until now to get it, one painful course at a time. Occasionally I've had to ask Craig for help, but I won't ever have to tell my little sister that I was too stupid to finish high school.

After I spend the morning cutting and painting baseboards for Hope House, Lauren and I take Hope to the playground. We buy ice cream at the concession stand, and then Hope takes my hand and leads me to the place on the beach where she often builds inuksuit with Celeste. It's the same stretch of beach I came to on the day I first arrived in Springdale. I remember the generous truck driver, how he gave money to a total stranger. I've been trying to pay it forward, as he asked, but it sure took me a while to get to it.

It's also the same beach where I tried to rebuild a relationship with Celeste. The weeping willow is huge now, and its branches sweep low over the beach. So many times it has provided me with shade and cover.

I'm impressed by how many inuksuit are here and that no one has come along and knocked them down. It reminds me of a scene back in Unity, that last spring before I fled. There'd been an entire community of them on the beach, some created by Craig though we had yet to meet him. Together, Lauren, Hope and I build another one before it's time to take her back to Abigail's, where she'll sleep for one last night.

Jimmy and Matthew are squeezed into a crowded corner of the kitchen, eating from paper plates piled high with food. Bowls and trays of food cover the table and all the counter surfaces. I fill a plate with potato salad, half a tuna-salad sandwich and a couple of Taviana's muffins and join them. "I'd say the Hope House opening is going well."

"No kidding," Jimmy says between bites.

"And Tavi's muffins are as good as ever," I say, snagging another one off the tray.

Through an ad in the local newspaper, the whole town of Springdale was invited to the grand opening of Hope House. Everyone we knew personally was asked to contribute food. They haven't let us down. There are also huge bouquets of flowers and balloons throughout the house. Someone from the local newspaper is milling about, taking pictures.

"Did you ever imagine this day would actually come?" I ask Jimmy.

He shakes his head. "All I initially wanted was to write a paper and get 90 percent or better. Who knew my idea could be made real? Not me. Now let's hope that the girls and women come."

"Build it and they will come," Matthew says.

"*Field of Dreams*," Jimmy replies.

I have no idea what they're talking about, though I've heard this line spoken a few times lately. "Speaking of hope," I say, trying to redirect the conversation, "have you seen our little guest of honor?"

"Oh yeah," Jimmy says. "She's dressed in her princess best and making the rounds. I'm afraid we've turned her into a little celebrity, and the attention has gone to her head."

Matthew and I laugh. "It'll be short-lived," I tell him.

"Hope-fully," Jimmy replies. "Pun intended."

"She may never really know what Celeste rescued her from," Matthew says. "Marriage at age fifteen. No education. Sister wives. Babies before she's fully grown herself."

"She'll figure it out," Jimmy says. "As she gets older."

"Did anyone hear from Selig?" I ask, changing the subject.

They both shake their heads. All of us have been trying to locate him, but without any luck. It's like he simply vanished the day he stepped onto the highway and put out his thumb. I figure that in this case, no news is bad news. If he'd landed on his feet he would have let us know. Abigail did her best for all of us, but in some cases, like his and almost mine, it was not enough.

When everyone's had a chance to mingle and eat, Alex directs us all onto the front lawn. "We have a presentation to make," he says.

This is news to me. I follow the crowd outside and see that Craig is rallying the crowd around the strange tarp-covered structure. When Alex is satisfied that everyone is there, he whistles to get the crowd's attention. The chatter dies away.

"Welcome, everyone, to the grand opening of Hope House!" A cheer goes up. It takes a moment before he can get the crowd quiet again. "We have a lot of people to thank today," he continues. "And we have an unveiling." He glances at the covered structure. "But first I'd like to introduce you all to the girl that Hope House is named after. Where are you, Hope?"

Alex scans the crowd. Hope breaks through the mob and runs up to him. Jimmy wasn't kidding. She really is dressed as a princess. I recognize the costume from Halloween. Her lips and face are sticky with the chocolate someone's given her. She beams up at her surrogate grandfather, who takes her hand and turns her to face the crowd. Another cheer goes up.

"Hope's mother, Celeste," Alex says, "chose this girl's name because she felt her baby daughter was going to provide hope to both her and other young mothers and girls in their community. Celeste wanted her daughter to have the kind of choices that she didn't have and a good education. Five years ago she made the brave decision to start a new life for herself and her young daughter here in Springdale." Alex hoists Hope onto his hip. "Jimmy, will you join us up here too?"

Jimmy moves through the crowd and stands beside Alex and Hope. His neck is crimson, and he looks at his feet.

Alex continues. "Jimmy met Celeste and Hope and saw the need to provide other girls and women like them with a place to turn to when they felt ready to leave their community. He researched the kind of support they would require and, well, got the ball rolling. That's how Hope House was first conceived, and in only three short years we have raised funds and established a home and refuge for these girls and women. Many services are now in place for these girls, and we look forward to welcoming them."

There's another loud cheer and more clapping from the crowd.

Alex puts Hope down and pulls a sheet of paper and his reading glasses from his shirt pocket. He begins to read from the list of private donors and local companies who helped renovate and set up the home. "We are a work in progress," he concludes, putting the list away. "We have charitable status and have set up a board of directors to overlook the running of Hope House. I'm *hoping*," he says with a grin, "that some of our young people from Unity will agree to sit on this board." His eyes meet mine. I think of Selig and am more sure than ever that I want to work to make a difference for both boys and girls leaving Unity.

"And now for the unveiling," Alex says. "One of our founding supporters, Craig Brandt, will take over from here."

Craig now steps up to address the crowd. Unlike Jimmy, he looks completely relaxed.

"Six years ago," he says, his voice clear and steady, "I was a high-school graduate with time on my hands." The crowd grows still, listening to his story. "I had no sense of direction or purpose. I often hung out at the river, both here and upstream, near Unity, building inuksuit and rock balances. I met Celeste on the beach, and we began creating inuksuit together. I explained to her how they were originally used by the Inuit people as directional markers. People made them to let those who came behind them know that they were on the right path. The inuksuit also signified safety, hope and friendship.

"Around that same time," he continues, "I met Jon while building inuksuit on the beach here in Springdale." He finds me in the crowd and smiles. "It was through my conversations with both Celeste and Jon that I began to discover my own life direction, which was to return to school—theology school. Soon Celeste had Hope and followed the direction that her own heart told her was right for her.

"So, Hope," he says, looking down at her, "I thought that an inuksuk at the front door of Hope House would be a perfect symbol to welcome girls who are choosing their life direction. Do you want to help me uncover it?"

Hope nods solemnly.

Craig begins releasing the bungee cords that hold the tarp down. When they have been placed aside, he holds the tarp on one side, and Hope holds it on the other. "One, two, three, lift!" he says.

The crowd cheers again.

The inuksuk is about seven feet high and built out of bricks. It's sturdy and strong, and even though it doesn't have a face, it looks friendly.

The live band resumes playing, and the formal part of the reception comes to an end. Children go back to playing games on the lawn, and their parents return to chatting with their neighbors.

Feeling deeply moved, I remain where I am, staring at the inuksuk, remembering all it took to get to this day. Celeste joins Craig beside it. She must not have known about it either. She's wiping tears from her face. Then she puts her hand in his, and he leans down to kiss her. It dawns on me that they're a couple and probably have been for a while. I don't know how I could have missed that.

A hand closes over mine. Lauren is beside me. "You okay?" she asks.

"Way more than okay," I say, putting my arm around her.

The crowd has gone. A small group of us have stayed behind to clean up. I find a child's picture book on a shelf in one of the bedrooms and lead a freshly bathed Hope into the living room so I can read her the story. It took a while, but I've come to value books, all kinds, and I want to be here to tuck her into her new bed. She snuggles up beside me on the couch, but after a few pages I realize her attention is not on the book, but on a car that has pulled up outside the house. Through the window I watch as a woman in a long, Unity-style dress steps out of the car and then reaches back inside to release a small child from a booster seat.

"Celeste," I call, without moving. "I think there's someone here you might know."

Celeste comes into the living room and watches as the woman takes bags out of the trunk. The driver doesn't get out to help her and pulls away as soon as she has gathered all her things. "Oh my god!" Celeste says, her eyes wide. "It's Pam!"

She runs out the front door, followed by Taviana. We watch as they take turns hugging the woman, and then Celeste and Taviana pick up the bags and lead her and the child inside. "This is my father's fifth wife, Pam," Celeste says. "She heard about Hope House from Taviana and—" Celeste is too choked up to continue.

"And now she's here!" Taviana declares. She wraps her arm firmly around Pam's waist. "Let me show you around."

Hope has stepped up to the little girl. They look so much alike, they could pass for twins. They gaze at each other for a moment and then, without saying a word, Hope reaches for the girl's hand and leads her down the hall.

I figure they must be cousins, but it gets so complicated in those families that I can't be sure.

"Build it and they will come," I mumble.

Craig looks at me. "Who was that driving?"

I can only shrug. "Someone who didn't want to be seen helping a girl leave Unity."

Craig thinks about that for a moment. "Have you ever heard of the underground railroad, Jon?"

I nod. I read about it in one of my history courses. There was no real railroad, only an underground organization of people willing to help black slaves escape to freedom by offering safe houses and secret routes. I realize what Craig is getting at.

"Do you think?" I ask.

"I have hope," he says, grinning.

Acknowledgments

With heartfelt gratitude to the members of my writing group—Diane Tullson and Kim Denman—for their never-ending support and encouragement. As well, my early readers gave me tremendously thoughtful feedback. Thank you Beryl Young, Deborah Hodge, Aaron Rabinowitz and Linda Irvine. Sara Cassidy, scrupulous editor, taught me how to tighten prose, and she put countless hours into fine-tuning the story. Thank you, Sara! And, as always, I am grateful to Orca Book Publishers, a collection of the nicest, most professional people you'll ever meet.

Although this is a work of fiction, I relied on many sources to help me better understand the plight of the lost boys of polygamy, but these three books were particularly invaluable in my research.

Lost Boy: The True Story of One Man's Exile from a Polygamist Cult and His Brave Journey to Reclaim His Life, by Brent W. Jeffs with Maia Szalavitz, Broadway Books, 2009.

The Secret Lives of Saints: Child Brides and Lost Boys in Canada's Polygamous Mormon Sect, by Daphne Bramham, Random House, 2008.

Stolen Innocence: My Story of Growing up in a Polygamous Sect, Becoming a Teenage Bride and Breaking Free of Warren Jeffs, by Elissa Wall with Lisa Pulitzer, HarperCollins, 2008.